Momentary Lapses of Reason

The Collected Short Stories

Hartley James

Table of Contents

Acknowledgements

Porcelain © 2002 First appeared in Fangoria 2002 writing as James A. Hartley
Memories of Home © 2019 First appeared in Just a Minor Malfunction November 2019 writing as Anthony James
Nature's Way first appeared in Electric Velocipede 2003.
Negative Density first appeared in Altair Magazine. 1999
Fairy Lights (Luci Fatate) first appeared in Nova SF Italy 1999
Fool's Luck first appeared in Colonies SF Magazine 2001
Raven's Eye first appeared in Flashing Swords 2005
Responsibility first appeared in Speculon 2001
Wings of the Gods © Hartley James 2021
Stone Feather first appeared in Altair Magazine 1998
The Bodysnatchin' Man first appeared in Challenging Destiny 1999
The Greening © Hartley James 2021
The Hero © Hartley James 2021
The Secret Properties of Glass © Hartley James 2021
Want first appeared in Naked Reader Press 2011
Water's Edge © Hartley James 2018

Porcelain

Dark eyes, slightly slanted, edged with porcelain. White rims tracing the curve, edged with gold. The face looked down at her. Only the face didn't look—it didn't move—just the eyes.

"She's awake," the voice spoke—quiet, sibilant. The china face muffled the sound.

A white oval surrounded by blackness was all she saw. Black eyes echoed the blackness behind.

"Do you think she's aware?" The other voice—male—came from behind her.

"Possibly. Too soon to tell.... Kara, Kara Donaldson. Can you hear me?"

Kara nodded her head. She tested her mouth with her tongue. It was dry, parched. She wanted a drink—a glass of water. She tried to moisten her mouth and throat by swallowing. Nothing would come. She tried to talk, to ask, but all she could manage was a feeble croak.

"No, don't try to talk. You aren't ready yet. Just rest," said the male voice behind her.

Questions were starting to form in the spaces of her half awareness. Where was she? What was happening to her? She felt a pressure against the top of her arm, then something sharp. More blackness, different this time, swept down upon her.

oOo

Awareness coalesced around her. She could feel the warmth and see the orange-pink glow of sunlight through her lids. The tracery of veins was there, darker in her sight. Kara barely dared to open her lids. She remembered last time, remembered the dry mouth and the confusion. Most of all, she remembered the faces. She clutched at the memory. Something about them. Faces that were faces and yet...

She opened her eyes. Wooden floorboards, shining, deep and rich with polish, led off to a fly screen door. She followed the lines of the boards, still blurry, but there all the same.

Outside.

Outside a tree waved in the wind. Leaves blew and rustled. The wooden-framed door creaked in the breeze. A swing seat hung on the veranda outside. The chain rubbed and clinked against wood. Summer. She knew it was summer. Late afternoon. The sunlight slanting through the door and the net curtains told her. The warmth and light told her.

Last thing Kara remembered was winter. How had it gotten to be summer without her knowing? She looked around the room, seeking clues to the holes in her memory. Something should tell her.

She turned beneath crisp, white sheets and chewed at her lower lip, willing the memory to come.

"Miss Donaldson, time to get up. You've been asleep for over an hour."

Kara looked slowly from the plain sensible shoes, up over stockinged legs and further, past a crisp, white dress. The face wore glasses perched upon the nose—a prim nose and a prim pink face to go with it.

"Miss Donaldson, come on, time to get up."

"Yes, yes. All right," said Kara. "I'm tired. Let me

rest."

"You've been asleep for too long already. If you don't get up now, you'll be awake half the night. Now, I won't ask you again."

Kara knew she should know this person, but the name wouldn't come. The woman's voice annoyed her, grating on her nerves. All she wanted was to go back to sleep. If she complied and sat up, perhaps the woman would go away. Kara felt hot. She ran her fingers through her hair, damp with sweat and sat up, working her tongue round her mouth.

"Water. Can you get me some water?"

"Good. That's more like it. Now I'll bring you a nice cool glass of lemonade. Would you like that instead, honey?" Kara narrowed her eyes at the woman and nodded. The woman gave a satisfied look and left the room.

Kara swung her legs out of the bed and put her feet on the floor. She wore a plain cotton shift and nothing else, nothing beneath it. She should know this place, know where she was, but the knowledge had gone, along with winter and spring. She looked around, at the room, at the bed, at the ceiling, where a fan rotated lazily through the torpid air. A fly buzzed and meandered through the heat.

The woman returned carrying a tall glass of lemonade. Ice clinked against the sides of the glass and condensation ran in tiny rivulets down its side. Kara licked her lips, took the glass and swallowed greedily.

"Mmm. God, I needed that." She took another long draft, then held the slick glass to her forehead and rubbed it from side to side. "Where am I?"

"Now, Miss Donaldson. One of these days, you're going to wake up and remember. One of these afternoons, you're going to wake and say 'Hello, Maysie, have I slept for long?' And yes, I know. That's going to be your next question, just like it always is. Maysie Fuller. That's my name. You've been here since the accident."

Kara looked out through the screen door as she digested the information. A dragonfly hovered over the veranda, then flicked away. She looked down at her legs, then her arms. Everything seemed to be in place. She didn't have any noticeable injury. She just couldn't seem to remember anything.

"Where am I? Is this a hospital?"

"No, Miss Donaldson. This is your place, left to you by Dr. Brightman." Maysie spoke as if it were a formula; something she had said many times before. "Now you finish that lemonade and get yourself up. I'll be back for the glass later."

Kara waited till Maysie had retreated, then placed the glass down gently on the bedside table. Carefully, she got to her feet, but it didn't seem like there was anything wrong. Her legs felt fine. The rest of her body felt fine. How could she have been in an accident?

She padded across the cool wood floor, barefoot, to the screen door and looked out. A large yard spread out before her. Long grass waved gently in the breeze and a massive fig tree stood in its own pool of shadow. She pushed open the screen door, winced a little as the springs creaked and protested, then stepped out onto the veranda. All around lay a sea of grass, as far as she could see.

Shielding her eyes from the beating sun, she stepped down the stairs to the ground. The grass, lush and moist against her bare feet, brushed like waves against her legs as she wandered through it, heading towards the tree. The shade offered by the wide, spreading branches looked inviting. Thankful for the solid trunk to lean her back against, she lowered herself to the ground. A centipede walked across the earth beside her, pushing past twigs and leaves, and she watched it, until it disappeared behind a large buttress root. She sat back in shadow and closed her eyes. The breeze was cool against her sweat-damp cheek.

"Hello, Miss Donaldson. How are we today?" Kara looked up to see a man in a white coat standing over her. He wore glasses, just like the woman. She guessed he was a doctor. He looked like a doctor.

"Um, fine, I guess. I don't know about you."

The man smiled at her. "Good. Glad to hear it. So how's the old memory going? Do you remember anything yet?"

She peered up at him. He had very blue eyes. The way he was talking to her, she was obviously meant to know who he was. The light was behind him, surrounding him. It was too bright and she had to squint. "I don't know. I have these 'flashes' of memory, but they don't seem to make any sense."

"Okay, well that's a start." He sat down beside her, his back against the exposed root. She could see him now. He had a good face, high brow, clean features. He was lightly tanned.

"Who are you? Are you a doctor? You look like a doctor." Kara tilted her head to one side and studied him.

He looked no different from that angle either.

"Just call me Alan, Miss Donaldson. We've met before, but I don't expect you'd remember yet." He smiled. "All in good time." His smile faded. "Can you tell me about these 'flashes' of yours?"

Kara thought about what she remembered. She rubbed her hand across her mouth and chin. That's right. Faces. White faces, hovering in the darkness. Faces, but not faces. Something about them. She rubbed the bridge of her nose and then her forehead.

"It's all right. Take your time."

Kara didn't trust him. He looked like the sort that you could trust, that you were supposed to trust. "I don't know. They're gone. I just sort of half remember them anyway. I don't think they're important."

He peered at her above his spectacles. "Anything is important Kara, anything at all. Just try and remember."

Kara leaned her head back against the tree trunk and closed her eyes. She wished he would go away. Cicadas croaked in the tree somewhere above her. When she opened her eyes again, he was gone. She hadn't heard him leave. She closed her eyes and tried to remember.

The images came slowly. She had to drag them out from some place buried deep within her. Eggshell white. Translucent. Kara reached out her fingers to touch, but the face withdrew. Blackness all around. Black like the black eyes. A vision hanging in the void.

The screen door slammed and Kara looked over to the house. Maysie stood in the shade of the veranda, hands on her hips. She stood there watching for a time, then turned and went back into the house. The screen door banged shut behind her. Kara looked at the wide wooden house. She looked at the sea of grass. She looked up at the clear blue sky. Suddenly, the cicada chorus stopped. Everything was so quiet. Only the wind whispered gently in her ears, in the leaves around her, and in the long grass. She pushed herself to her feet and headed back towards the house.

oOo

Awareness fluttered at the back of Kara's consciousness. She reached out to touch it, but gossamer thin, it dissolved beneath her questing grasp. She was hot, the pillow damp beneath her cheek. She wanted a drink.

"Miss Donaldson, time to get up. You've been asleep for over an hour."

Kara worked her mouth, trying to moisten it. She licked her dry lips and opened her eyes, gritty with sleep. She turned her head to look at the ceiling fan, rotating lazily through the heat above her. She tracked the motion of the blades. Round and round and round. What had she been dreaming about? Something about faces, white faces—or faces half covered by things like masks. The drink could wait.

"Miss Donaldson, come. Time to get up."

Kara continued watching the fan. She answered without turning her head.

"Not today, Maysie. Not today."

How had she known the woman's name? It had just been there. Other things were there, dim shapes behind the curtain of her memory. They waited for her there, just out of her reach, and she wanted them.

Kara turned her head, but Maysie had gone. A fly buzzed through the thick air, then landed somewhere out of sight. All was still. She pulled back the crisp, white sheets and swung her legs round and out of bed, to place her feet on the cool wood floor. The smooth polished boards felt good against her bare soles. She sat, the heels of her hands pressed against the edge of the bed. Her hair fell in sweat-damp strings around her face. She sat there thinking, trying to remember. Nothing would come but fleeting images that skittered away from her—images, and a smell; a smell like a hospital. Neither made any sense at all. Taking a deep breath, she stood and walked across the room and over to the screen door.

Without thinking about it, she knew the springs would creak in protest when she opened it. She pushed it open, stepped outside and let it bang shut behind her, not caring about the noise. A sea of grass waved in front of her, as far as the eye could see. She moved out from the shaded veranda and took the three steps to the ground. The grass was long even here, right up to the side of the house. Shielding her eyes from the glare, she moved through the grass towards the pool of shade beneath the tree. A dragonfly crossed her path, hovered for an instant, then flicked away. Kara watched until it was out of sight, then headed towards the shade and sat, her back against the broad, smooth trunk. Alan came then, as she knew he would.

"Hello, Miss Donaldson. How are we today?"

Kara peered up at him. She narrowed her eyes. He waited patiently, unmoving, waiting for her to answer.

"Not today. I don't want to answer your questions.

I have things to do."

He tilted his head a little to one side and stood above her looking puzzled. Kara moistened her lips and stared at him. She stared at his face and eyes. They were too perfect, too right. She concentrated on his features. It may have been her imagination, but the brightness behind him grew just a fraction. She continued to stare.

A piece of his face cracked off and fell to the ground at his feet. Then another. The shards of his face fell like flakes of rust, until there was nothing left but a clean white surface. Dark eyes looked down at her, dark eyes edged with gold.

"Not today," she said to the blank white mask. "I have things to do."

She leaned her head back against the tree trunk and closed her eyes. When she opened them again, he was gone. She looked out across the grass. She didn't have long to wait. One by one, the others came and walked towards her. She looked up at their faces and smiled at them.

"We have things to do," she said. "We all have things to do. Now is the time to show them how."

Kara got to her feet, a smile still on her face, and headed out across the sea of grass, not even checking to see if they followed.

oOo

Dr. Alan Bright looked down at the still form in the bed before him. Wires trailed from the electrodes fastened to her temples and from beneath the crisp, white sheets to the monitors above the bed. Everything was going to plan. Similar beds lay behind him and to either side, twelve in all. In each lay one of the volunteers. He smiled down at Kara, glanced up at the monitor, then looked back at her sleeping face. She could have been asleep, but he knew she wasn't.

"Well, Kara. We're nearly there. Just a few more days and the trial will be over. Then you can get back to whatever sort of life you were leading before." He smiled. "Six months is a long time, but you'll get there. You only have to wait a few more days."

Kara Donaldson opened her eyes and looked at him. Dr. Bright blinked in disbelief, then sucked in his breath. Dark, dark eyes stared at him from the pale white face beneath Kara's shaven head. She licked her lips. Her eyes continued staring at him, through him.

"Not today, Alan. I have things to do," she said. "*We* all have things to do. No time to wait."

But this was impossible! Bright's mouth hung open in shock as Kara closed her eyes again. He stared at her, barely able to move. How could she have spoken? He shook his head. No. Then, just as he was about to reach over and check her, the monitor above her bed stopped its steady pulse—a hiccup, followed by an even, high-pitched, unbroken tone.

One by one, above every bed around the room, the monitors ceased their steady pulse. One by one, the sound of his patients' heartbeats faded to nothing. One by one, they joined together in that single, even, unbroken, high-pitched tone.

And with that sound, he knew.

Slowly Bright lifted a hand to his mouth.

"Oh my God," he said.

oOo

The springs creaked in protest as the screen door moved slightly in the breeze. It banged, once, twice against the wooden frame. Around the broad house, a sea of grass stirred lazily in the breeze, moving in gentle waves as far as the eye could see. The grass was long even here, right up to the side of the house. Out along the path, a dragonfly hovered for an instant, then flicked away, fading rapidly to become a mere rainbow glimmer in the distance.

The sun beat down, warm across the long-grassed fields. At the end of the path, in the shade of a large, smooth-trunked tree, a centipede walked across the earth, pushing past twigs and leaves, finally to disappear behind a large buttress root. In front of the tree, in a recently disturbed patch of dirt, a small pile of rusted flakes sat alone, unwatched, undisturbed, beneath the spreading leaves.

-The End-

Memories of Home

"I don't know who the fuck you think you're working for, and I don't really care. The truth is..." Kavanagh leaned in closer, shaping each word clearly, concisely. "…you work for me."

He watched the impact, judged the expression in the young man's eyes. He'd seen the sequence enough times in the past. First the resentment, the affront, then the traces of uncertainty and finally a vague touch of fear. He turned away, scanning the cabin for anything he might be able to use, more out of habit than need, but Nash kept his quarters clean and free from clutter. Really, Kavanagh had the younger man, Nash, where he wanted him.

"Now, if you understand that relationship, we'll be fine. This is not about you. It's about what we have to do. You see, I'm going to need you, and Vaylorus is as important as any of these new worlds from the old Union. The problem is, they're a little inclined to go off on their own. It's our job to reel them back in."

"But— "

"What?" said Kavanagh.

"I'm supposed to be reporting to--"

"Did you not hear me?" said Kavanagh.

Nash swallowed and bit his lip.

"Good. Now, we're due to land in two days' time, so I suggest you use that period to think about your priorities. You can have a career, or you can end up stuck on this god-forsaken fringe world for the rest of your existence. Your choice."

Nash closed his eyes, and after a pause, opened them again and nodded. Satisfied for the moment, Kavanagh gave him one last assessing look, held it for an instant, then slipped out of the cabin.

One day, they might be able to get from place to place without the dead, useless time between. Not that he had any real interest in the places the Confederacy decided had need of his presence. He just liked to be engaged.

Derek Nash. The young man was smart, one of the rising stars. His direct superiors relied on him, and already gave him fair latitude to make his own decisions. Useful. After all, there were agendas and there were agendas. If he could rely on Nash to perform, there'd be one less problem to worry about, and he'd have less time to spend on the stinking ball that was Vaylorus. Since the collapse of the Union, everything had more or less fallen apart. Problem was that the resources were too valuable for the Confederacy to ignore.

Once back in his own cabin, Kavanagh settled back on the couch, thumbed the wall screen into life, and returned to the studying the Go board where he'd left it. His move.

oOo

Vaylorian immigration was worse than he remembered it. Kavanagh walked up the long connecting ramp, hearing it creak and shift beneath his feet with every step. The wind slammed against the thin metallic walls in gusts that shuddered and rocked the structure. The cold bit through, making him quicken his pace, trying to get into the terminal building as quickly as possible. They disembarked into a vast echoing chamber, barely lit, the outside snow swirling across the windows and obscuring the landscape, not that there was much to see. Vast, frigid, forested plains, draped in white and not much else was out there. The spaceport was miles out from Sira Kalrim, stuck in the middle of nowhere.

The smell of fuel and metal swept over him as he stepped, finally, thankfully, into the warmth and looked for some indicator of which way he should be heading. There was something else in the air as well, some acrid, ammoniac scent that he finally recognized as the under taste of poorly maintained rest rooms. The Vaylorians never seemed to notice such things – their olfactory mechanisms were apparently put together differently.

He was thankful, at least, that they were the only ship coming in at this time. He remembered the queues from last time, and grimaced. He could never quite understand why anyone would want to come here as a tourist, but come they did. Despite that small blessing, it turned out to be bad enough. One by one, they filed up toward the border control booths and formed an orderly line. He scanned the other passengers. A few corporate types, looking just about as impressed as he felt and the inevitable pack of wide-eyed tourists. Tourism, it seemed, was one of the things that was starting to keep the place alive.

Kavanagh dropped his bag at his feet, ready for the wait as one after the other, the uniformed officials went through the motions of checking paperwork, taking their own precious time. It was funny how they still called it paperwork. A line of booths formed a barrier across the width of the vast echoing hall, each one populated with a Vaylorian official in ill-fitting drab uniforms. Their large bulk filled the booths, barely giving them space to do anything else but check the arrivals, each in ordered turn. Covered in mottled grey-black fur, they stood almost as wide as they were tall, vast rolls of insulating flesh thinly concealed beneath their military-style uniforms. The design of their clothing suggested a hangover from Union days, and the carefully controlled pacing was reminiscent of the regimentation left by Union on this, among many similar worlds, before the collapse.

At last, it was his turn, and he stepped up to the booth and handed over his datacard to the official. She took the thin sliver and turned it over and over in her claws, then after an appropriate level of time had passed, slipped it into the reader. Her huge dark eyes stared down at the reader disinterestedly. Her broad fleshy lips worked, gently twitching at the edges as she processed the information on the screen in front of her. The pungent fur smell of the Vaylorian female washed over him, and he did all he could to resist wrinkling his nose.

She kept him standing there a full twenty minutes, looming over him, occasionally glancing from side to side, checking the progress of her fellow officials before grudgingly letting him pass. He knew it was all show, all routine. They had a quota and went at a pre-defined pace – yet another way of pretending decent employment levels -- but it annoyed him all the same. The last look she gave him was one he read as belligerent hostility above her wide, soft-lipped mouth and he could feel the suspicion drilling into his back as he headed to the customs area to pick up the rest of his bags.

Nash finally joined him at the delivery point, looking tired and frustrated already.

"Is it always like this?" Nash asked.

Kavanagh gave a brief unamused laugh. "We're here on a good day. You'll see. Wait until we get into Sira Kalrim. Let's just hope the local boys have sent someone to meet us. Last time I had to try to negotiate transport into the city. There'd been some screw up and they'd forgotten to send someone to pick me up. Not fun. You'll soon learn. Whatever they told you before they gave you this assignment, well, there are truths, and there are truths. You'd better get used to it though. You've got a couple of years here, right?"

Kavanagh stooped to grab his other bag as the delivery cart trundled to a stop in front of them, not waiting for Nash's answer.

"Better you than me," he said as he straightened and waited for Nash to get his own luggage. "And make sure you've got your hat. You're going to need it. Head, hands, and feet. That's the litany. Remember it."

Maybe if Kavanagh had been younger, he would have jumped at an opportunity like this one, taken an assignment on some inhospitable border world as a path to quick advancement, but he liked his comforts these days. Besides, he'd seen enough of these places. After a while, they all started to fade, one into the other. Vaylorus, though, was special. It occupied a unique, unpleasant place in his heart.

As he led Nash through customs and into the transport area, into the human cluster of pinched white faces and bulky thermals, he was relieved to see a sign further back with his name misspelled in big clear letters. Even that didn't matter. This time, they'd been kind enough to send a driver. It was a Vaylorian driver, but it was a driver.

oOo

"You done much research on the place?" Kavanagh asked as they settled back into the transport for the three-hour journey into the city and beyond. There was going to be precious little communication from their driver, an old warrior, if the scars across his shoulders were anything to go by. He wondered briefly if the driver had been involved in the struggle against Union. It would do no good to ask. Kavanagh doubted that the creature could even understand them. The smell of half-damp fur and mud permeated the space.

"Research? Yes, I think I know enough," said Nash, watching the blank white landscape slide past the windows, and still shivering slightly from his exposure to the outside.

"Don't fool yourself. There's never enough. And there's no substitute for local knowledge, no matter how well informed you think you are. Jesus, if I was here for more than a few weeks even, I'd want to know everything I could about the place."

Nash leaned forward in his seat, looking at something outside the window. "What are they?" he asked, pointing out some hulking, snow-covered shapes by the roadside.

"See, there's an example," said Kavanagh. "There are some things that your company guidebooks aren't going to show you. They're old ground transports."

"But what--?"

"What are they doing out here? Oh, it's simple. When the economy nose-dived before the Union fell apart completely, it got too expensive to lay a hand on the parts. If something broke down, they just left it there. Been going on for years. There's been no reason to clean them up."

A particularly heavy jolt shook the vehicle and Kavanagh thrust out a hand. Nash grimaced as he banged his head on the window next to him.

"Just like the roads," said Kavanagh, with a grin. "At least they pick up the bodies."

Nash turned to look at him briefly, then turned back to face the walls of thick, purple-trunked trees, branches sagging under a weight of heavy snow. The trees were the reason anyone even cared about this place. Despite advances in technology and production, power-generation still mattered. The forested ice ball supported a self-sustaining fuel source the like of which was unequalled in the system anymore. Up until the collapse, Union had held a nicely wrapped up monopoly. Now, the only way Vaylorus was going to survive was on Confederacy finance. For the past few years, the central body had been pumping funds into Sira Kalrim, trying to prop up the local operations at the centre.

Sometimes, it took just a little persuasion for the locals to understand the economic reality.

Union had concentrated on Sira Kalrim, the hub of the most densely forested continent. Around that landmass stretched vast ice seas, broken only by random outcroppings of towering rock-strewn islands, upon which little of any use grew. Vaylorus, in essence, *was*

Sira Kalrim. Other than that, Kavanagh had no interest in the place at all.

He turned back to watch Nash, assessing. Maybe he'd be all right, maybe he wouldn't. The next few days would tell.

oOo

Sira Kalrim displayed its usual pallid illumination and forbidding architecture as their vehicle drew into the main thoroughfare. Union had been very big on statues and monumental edifices. The buildings in the capital *loomed.* All around their own vehicle, others transports wove in and out in various states of disrepair, grinding and growling in every direction. If there were any rules to the traffic flow, Kavanagh had never been able to work them out. He'd hate to have to drive here. Mud spattered across the windows and quickly froze, only to drop off the front screen, cut away by the heavy motorized blades.

"Big, isn't it?" said Kavanagh.

"It is that," breathed Nash.

"Yeah, it got me like that the first couple of times I was here. The feeling never truly goes away. Wait until they get you set up in your apartment. They're like these ones out here. Huge heating pipes inside and padded metal doors leading into every living space. They're supposed to keep out the noise, but they never really do. Not the sound of the heating, nor of the occasional shooting, but you'll get used to it soon enough. My own personal belief is that the doors are there to keep out the other Vaylorians. I really hope they've given you a decent package."

Nash tore his gaze away from the passing buildings long enough just to shoot a narrow-eyed glance in Kavanagh's direction. As he turned back to watch, he sighed.

"Listen," he said still gazing out the window. "I'm not quite sure what you're trying to do, scare me, make me change my mind or what. I took this assignment with my eyes wide open. I have no expectations, and I'm looking forward to the experience. The culture, the history, the parallels with old Earth fascinate me—there's just so much to learn here. That might not appeal to you, Mr Kavanagh, but I want to experience as much as I can while I still can. I took this job to get their procedures and processes in order and to provide as much assistance as I am able. Anything I can do to help them clamber out of their current state...well, I feel totally justified in doing it. That's my brief. That's what I want to achieve here. You may have some agenda of your own, but I'm going to do what I can to help Vaylorus and the Confederacy at the same time. No one has to lose here."

Good for you, Nash, thought Kavanagh. Perhaps he'd work out after all.

oOo

One of the old Union rally buildings, places where the local population had gathered to debate and growl at each other across the vast central space. Housed their offices now. Historically, the debates in these places would turn into actual physical combat, Union representatives clustered around, waiting to see which principle prevailed. Other times, the differences of opinion were settled by extended drinking contests. Never go drinking with a Vaylorian. Kavanagh had learnt that one pretty quickly.

As they pulled into the front of the building, Kavanagh reached into his bag and pulled out a bottle. He leaned over the front and shook it from side to side beside their driver. The Vaylorian took a moment to notice, turned, and with a brief growling noise, shook his head. Kavanagh persisted, waving the bottle again. With a grunt, their driver nodded and clutched it between his claws.

"What's that all about?" said Nash.

"Something you'd do well to learn," said Kavanagh. "Protocol doesn't allow gratuities, but it never hurts. Never know when you're going to need a favour out here. You'll find yourself relying on these guys pretty soon. Don't expect to find any sort of easy transportation. Wait until you have to make a trip out to one of the mills, or the extraction plants. The plants are generally in the middle of some frozen waste. Personally, I like staying alive."

Nash just looked thoughtful. Kavanagh was feeling increasingly comfortable with the young man. He didn't give much away and very little that Kavanagh had thrown at him so far had seemed to fluster him.

They clambered out of the vehicle together, carrying their bags, thermal coats buttoned to their necks, and flaps lowered on their headgear. Wide, glass and metal, dirt-streaked doors concealed a murky interior. Already their vehicle had shuddered away. Kavanagh pushed open one of the doors and led them inside. The poorly lit interior echoed with their steps. The smell of sweaty boilers and tree-fuel heating wafted over them in a wave of warmth. A popular song drifted through the hollow space, playing off somewhere in the distance and echoing off the walls, slightly distorting the sound. Kavanagh recognized it as a popular tune from the system charts a few years ago, "Memories of Home," and it brought a slightly amused grin to his lips at the incongruity. Sometimes it took years before some of the trends in music and culture filtered out to these worlds. Memories of home – on Vaylorus? He grinned inwardly at the irony.

Over in one corner stood a Vaylorian security officer, stun prod in hand, rocking slightly back and forth. The Vaylorian saw them standing there, stripping off their coats and hats, and quickly snapped to alert, his shoulder hair bristling. Before the guard had a chance to think about it, Kavanagh had stepped across, waving his ID high. Still bristling, the guard peered down. Kavanagh waved Nash forward.

"Quick, show him your ID," he said.

The Vaylorian took a few moments, processing, and then visibly relaxed, his shoulder hairs settling back down. He gestured up a staircase with his stun prod and a low growl.

As they mounted the staircase, Kavanagh spoke to Nash in a low voice. "When you walk into a building, show them who you are as quickly as you can. They're suspicious as anything, and there's a tension between the Vaylorians and the human ex-pats that isn't going to go away in a hurry. A lot of them blame us for the collapse of their economy and anything else they can think of. When you think that Union was basically human, you can understand why. There's still quite a few of the old guard around, and you never know."

"How long have you spent here before?" asked Nash.

"Long enough."

They climbed the rest of the staircase in silence, Kavanagh aware that Nash was watching him speculatively. They climbed two floors, headed through another set of glass doors, and with a sense of relief, Kavanagh led Nash through into the human part of the offices.

There was no reception, no one to greet them, but Kavanagh knew where he was going. He threaded his way between desks and cubicles, heading for the large set of offices at the end of the floor. He knocked once on a large door, and without waiting for a response, stepped inside, gesturing for Nash to follow him.

Inside, the office was furnished to the barest minimum. Behind a desk sat a very harassed looking, grey-faced man, his receding hairline revealing more pale flesh than white-flecked hair. The man looked up as the pair of them entered.

"Kavanagh! Ouch, I forgot you were coming in today. Welcome. Welcome." He stood and stepped around the desk, hand extended. "You got here no problem? Good."

"Hello, Sam. This is— "

"Yes, I know. It's Nash, isn't it? Welcome. Welcome. I'm glad you made it."

"Pleased to meet you, Mr Goldberg. I'm very pleased to be here. I hope that we can do some good here together. I'm really looking forward to working with you."

Goldberg fussed around, pulling out chairs. "Sit. Sit, please. Can I get you a drink or something? How was your trip?"

"No, we're fine," said Kavanagh. "I'd like to talk about what's been happening."

"Yes, yes. Of course, you would." He leaned back on the edge of the desk. "You've arrived none too soon. Both of you. Relations with the local hierarchy have become very tense. They're pushing for more authority, more ownership. You know how it's always been. Well, now for some reason, they're becoming very demanding."

"Have you met with the local senior office holders?" asked Nash, leaning forward in his chair.

Kavanagh waved him down and narrowed his eyes. "We've been here before, Sam. And, well, they're just going to have to learn, aren't they? If they start messing with the Confederacy, we'll just pull support. They'll soon wake up then."

"I don't think it would be a very good idea to threaten them," said Goldberg. "I'd prefer to handle this gently. You forget; I've been here on the ground. Lately, their negotiations have been a little more aggressive. No…a lot more." He sighed and ran his hand over his forehead. "It seems they believe they can run the whole operation without Confederacy support. I've had rumours of discussions with the home-grown human population as well. Not good. Not good at all."

"What good's that going to do them?" said Kavanagh. "Why on earth would the local community want to side with them anyway?"

"I do really think we should listen to what they have to say," said Nash.

This time Kavanagh gave him a pointed frown. Confederacy operations had been set up on Vaylorus as a joint venture with the local hierarchy as lip service to local sensibilities, not because they needed the Vaylorian management. The creatures were starting to get above themselves. It was Nash's job to enforce procedure and systems, not to enter into some sort of mission in public relations and good works.

"I hear what you're saying, Nash," said Kavanagh. "Mister Goldberg here has the real local knowledge. I'm sure your suggestions are made with the very best intention, but that's not the priority here. What matters is making sure we have as little trouble with the locals as possible and meanwhile maintaining as much smooth and profitable production as we can. Do you have a problem with that? Is anything about that unclear? Because if it's not clear...."

"No. I understand you perfectly," said Nash, quietly.

Kavanagh nodded, steepled his fingers in front of his face and thought for a moment.

"All right, Sam. What Nash says does make some sort of sense. We need to meet with the Vaylorian contingent. It's time we made it very clear to them what's what. How long would it take you to set up a meeting?"

"Oh, an hour or so. Yes. An hour, maybe a little more. Depending on how many of their leadership are in the building, but two hours at most. We should be able to get enough of them who matter."

"Good. Let's do it."

oOo

It was like something out of the pictures Kavanagh had seen of Vaylorian history. On one side of the vast central meeting area stood the Vaylorian contingent. On the other stood the humans. Numbers were roughly even, but because of the Vaylorian body size, Kavanagh felt like they were outnumbered at least two to one. If that was not bad enough, they had to maintain the protocols. You were meant to sit in meetings, not stare across a dim, open, echoing space like two hostile tribes.

Sam Goldberg stepped into the centre of the circle, facing the local leadership looking nervous and twitchy. On the other side, the Vaylorian shoulder hair was going up and down randomly. Wide fleshy mouths opened and shut, and wrinkled brows furrowed. Goldberg had been right; it was just a little tenser than he had imagined. Why couldn't they have proper, human, meetings?

Goldberg cleared his throat, and the sound echoed around the chamber.

"Thank you all for coming on such short notice," he said. "The reason I've called this meeting is to introduce Mr Kavanagh from Central Office. Some of you will have met him before, but he is here today with a specific purpose. Confederacy leadership is concerned about the adoption of a new set of policies and procedures. Mr Kavanagh has brought with him a new member of our local delegation, Mr Derek Nash. It will be Mr Nash's responsibility to work beside you to implement the new systems and make sure that all procedure is followed."

There were low grumbles from across the other side of the circle. Goldberg ignored them and continued.

"Yes, well. We are lucky to have someone like Mr Kavanagh with us. Perhaps he would like to say a few words."

Kavanagh nodded, thanked Goldberg, and stepped to the centre of the circle.

He held the moment, scanning the alien faces arrayed across from him. A whisper of warm tree-fuel breeze stirred across the chamber. There was a grunt and further around the circle, another of the creatures shifted its bulk.

"As Sam rightly says, some of you will know me. And I'm sure you will understand how important the Confederacy feels that Vaylorus and Sira Kalrim really are. It's for that reason that I am here." Kavanagh had no clue if he'd be able to tell which of the Vaylorians that little piece of information might possibly apply to. He waited, letting the statement sink in before continuing.

"We at Central Office have recently had some concerns about production quotas, about costs and overheads. We believe that things could be run a little more efficiently and that would benefit all of us. Nash is here to make sure that happens, and we have developed a set of systems and procedures meant to maximize the benefit to us all. I'm sure you're all aware, that without the Confederacy's funding to support your failing infrastructure after the Union collapse, that you would have been completely unable to run anything here on Vaylorus. Without our support today, you would be unable to continue your operations – I don't think I need to tell you what that would mean for Vaylorus "

"Wrong!" The loud growl came from one of the Vaylorians. There was a deep grumble of assent.

"I think you'll find— "

"No!"

"What? Do you want the Confederacy to withdraw all its resources? Because that's what you're risking. You understand that?"

"Oh, we understand that very well." Nash's voice, from behind him. He whirled as the young man stepped forward to join him in the circle's centre.

"What do you think you are doing?" said Kavanagh from between tightly closed teeth.

"I'm doing precisely what we've been planning for some time," said Nash calmly. "We thank the Confederacy for many things. We thank it for the funding, for the training, for the support it has given to those of us born and raised on Vaylorus. We are very grateful for the Confederacy's assistance in moving us through the transition that we faced after the dissolution of Union."

Nash walked past him and moved to stand in front of the assembled Vaylorians.

Kavanagh watched him with narrowed eyes. "But I don't understand. What do you think you're doing, Nash?"

The young man took three steps forward. Two of the large creatures waddled forward to stand on either side of him.

"I was born here on Vaylorus, Mr Kavanagh. I've seen our people struggle here, both human and Vaylorian. I've watched us climb through the slush and the mud and the oppression. Union did a lot of damage here, but it also did a lot of good. It taught the human population and the Vaylorians how to work together to survive. Years ago, when I was old enough, I left, as did many of the others who could get out. I'm Vaylorian, Kavanagh. You seem to forget that there are two populations here, have been for decades. Human and Vaylorian have lived together side by side for all that time. And at last, I, and many others, have finally come home. Many of us took positions with Confederacy companies, obscured the fact of where we came from. You know, it's funny. Most of the time, companies didn't really care where we came from apart from the leverage it might give them in some place or another."

There was a long pause while Kavanagh processed what the young man was saying, and then Nash continued.

"We thank the Confederacy for the training, for the support, for the investment to enable us to be where we are, to become self-sufficient. But now it's time for the bureaucrats to leave."

"You can't!" said Kavanagh. "You can't do this. You work for us. How come I had no knowledge that you were Vaylorian? Anyway, that shouldn't matter. I think you'd better forget this stupidity now if you know what's good for you."

Nash looked at him impassively. "You know, Kavanagh," he said. "There's never enough research. And there's no substitute for local knowledge, no matter how well informed you think you are. I think those were your words, weren't they?"

"But..."

"It's time for you to go home now," said Nash. "It's also time for Mr Goldberg and many of the others to go home. We'll make sure they get out of here safely, but they'd better do it quickly. I already am home. This *is* my home. I'm quite sure your driver will make sure you get back to the spaceport safely. The ship out won't be leaving for at least another day."

"Do you really think you can ...?"

"Have a safe trip, now. Your transport's waiting for you downstairs. I wouldn't stay around too long if I were you. The others will have to the end of the week. But then…" He shrugged.

The two very large Vaylorians standing on either side of Nash quickly bristled. Kavanagh swallowed once, his mind racing. One of the Vaylorians took a step forward.

Suddenly feeling very nervous, Kavanagh started moving rapidly for the door.

Behind him, Nash was humming something as he walked back into the offices. With a grimace, Kavanagh realized that he recognized the song. It was *Memories of Home*.

Where was the irony now?

-The End-

Nature's Way

The slither hound was pregnant. The swell of spore tickled beneath her flowing tresses. Of course, she didn't know she was a slither hound. That was just what the others called her, the strangers. She scanned the horizon and snuffed at the air, searching for a hint of ungulate, but the taste of ungulate on the gentle breeze that stirred the slim stalks around her was missing. It had been a long time since she had smelled the tang of the huge herbivores on the air. She rippled her multiple tiny legs and shifted position, sensing. The ground lay still beneath her.

Since the coming of the strangers, the ground had been still more often than not. It had not caused her too much concern up to now. The land teemed with insects and the small wriggling larvae she liked to feed on, but the steps of the larger beasts had been strangely absent. Now, with her burgeoning spore, her needs were different.

She shifted position again, seeking movement, testing the air and listening. Sound and taste guided her mostly. Her large brown eyes were adequate at close range, but with her head so close to the ground, they were little use at a distance. Her multiple sensitive feet helped, picking up vibration from the ground beneath her.

Her ears pricked up as she noticed noises

from beyond the rise in front. Perhaps there she would find what she needed. With a low keening deep in her throat, she shot to the top of the low hill.

oOo

"What the hell was that?"

"What?" Luke looked over at his client with a barely disguised frown. He liked this one less than most, but the man was paying the bills.

"That noise?" Janus Margate was peering down his rifle sights and scanning the horizon.

"Nothing to worry about. Probably just a slither hound, Mister Margate. You don't get many of them, but they're pretty harmless."

Margate snorted, lowered his rifle and rested it in the crook of one arm. Multi-pocketed khakis and a slouch hat completed the image. Most of his clients liked to dress the part. He lifted his water bottle and took a healthy swallow. "So where are these animals that are supposed to be here? You promised me big game. Nothing for two whole days. Perhaps I should just bag one of these slither hound things and call it quits."

Luke crouched down in the long reddish grass and sighed quietly. "I don't think you'd want that, Mister Margate. They look kind of like a short Cocker Spaniel. I doubt you'd *really* want that in your trophy room."

Margate snorted and went back to scanning the horizon. "Well, something had better happen soon. I've paid you good money, McEvoy, and damned if you're not going to deliver."

Luke rubbed the back of his neck and grimaced. Margate was within his rights to be annoyed. He plucked a grass stalk and turned it between his fingers. There'd been no sign of the large bison-like creatures they'd come hunting for a full two days. Migratory patterns should have dictated they'd be here, but so far nothing. Luke wondered what had changed to cause them to alter their seasonal movement. They'd been here every year for the last six seasons. What had changed now?

The slither hound's low keening came from a nearby hill. Luke turned, but there was little chance of seeing the creature in this long grass. He pushed himself to his feet, brushed off his hands and crossed to stand behind his red-faced client. He stared at the man's bull neck and phrased his next statement carefully.

"Listen, Mister Margate. If there's no sign of them by sundown, we'll break camp and head to another spot I know. I'm sorry, but that waterhole is usually a good bet. I don't know why we've had no activity yet."

Margate grunted and peered over at the waterhole. Nothing. Nothing more than a few lizbirds spiraling lazily above the water and hopping around the muddy edges. Six seasons and he'd never seen the place so quiet. He'd spent too long building up his lucrative one-man business to see it all going wrong now.

"Humph," said Margate. "Seems like there's a lot you don't know."

Margate was clearly unimpressed, but there was nothing he could say to the man.

A sudden rustling from somewhere nearby spun them both around. A wave of motion was bearing down on them, snaking through the long grass.

"What the —?" said Margate. He took a step back. Then another - slamming right into Luke who stood directly behind. The big man went flying, his rifle spinning off to one side.

"Arghh, you idiot!" Margate yelled as he went down. Then, "Ooof," as he hit the ground and the air was driven from his lungs.

Whatever it was cutting through the grass made straight for him. A slither hound shot from beneath the concealing grass, leaped from the ground and landed right on Margate's chest. It rested on top of him, looking down at his face with its big brown eyes, quivering slightly.

Margate looked petrified. His big face had gone pale and he held himself rigid, staring at the creature perched on top of him. "What should I do?" he forced from between clenched teeth, barely daring to move.

Luke, trying very hard not to explode with laughter at the sight told him. "Nothing. I told you, they're harmless, Mister Margate. It'll get bored in a minute and then it'll be gone."

"Get the damn thing off me!"

The slither hound gave a low keening cry, then proceeded to shake itself. It was not unlike a wet dog, shaking its coat free of water. Long tresses whipped from side to side and a cloud of dust enveloped both the animal and the man who lay beneath. It stood quivering for a moment more, then shot away again, into the concealment of the long grass. A second later and there was no trace of it. Margate lay where he had fallen, his eyes wide.

Still suppressing his urge to laugh, Luke bit his lip and crossed to help Margate up.

As Luke hoisted his client to his feet, Margate found his voice again. "There'll be hell to pay for this, McEvoy. Hell to pay." He proceeded to brush down his clothes, sending up fine puffs of brown dust. "What was that thing? Look at this, it's left dirt all over me," he growled. "I'm telling you McEvoy, if —"

Luke turned away so Margate couldn't see his face. "That was the fearsome slither hound, Mister Margate. I'm sorry that your dignity's been compromised, but it's perfectly harmless."

"Dignity! Why I — "He spluttered, then stalked off to retrieve his rifle.

Luke pressed his lips together tightly and

turned to watch the big man. The slither hound was certainly harmless

– as far as he knew. He'd never seen one do anything like that before, but he was glad he'd been here to see it now. The memory of Margate's face was going to stay with him for a long, long time. He'd seen enough of the corporate types who came on these hunting trips over the past six seasons. They didn't give a damn about the countryside or the beauties of this outpost world. All they cared about was another set of trophies to massage their over-inflated egos.

Margate was stalking back towards him, swinging his rifle with one hand and brushing at his shirt with the other. By the looks of him, there'd be no more hunting for the rest of the day. If nothing else, it gave Luke an excuse to shift to a new campsite where they'd have better prospects. He scanned the horizon and nodded to himself.

"Well?" said Margate.

Luke gave him a slight frown and tilted his head in query.

"Well, what are you going to do?" said Margate, looking flustered.

"About what, Mister Margate?"

"About that damn animal, that's what?"

"What would you like me to do?"

Margate grumbled to himself then dropped his gaze. "All right then. What now?"

"I suggest we shift camp, Mister Margate. We

can head for that other location I told you about. I think we'll have a better chance there. It's about a day's drive, but there are some great sights along the way. We can start first thing in the morning and be ready for a full day's hunting the day after tomorrow with an early start."

"Scenery! What do I want with scenery? I came to this God-forsaken place to hunt. So far, there's been precious little of that. It's about time you started earning your keep, McEvoy."

"We'll see what we can do then," said Luke. "But let's just call it a day now and head back to the campsite."

It took them about forty minutes to make their way back. Margate strode beside him with a face like thunder, muttering to himself under his breath. Luke ignored the performance. It was just one more thing he was paid to put up with.

It was strange they'd seen none of the veldt bulls in the grasslands around the waterhole. He could think of nothing that would cause them to change their pattern after so many seasons. Perhaps they'd have more success at the next location. They'd better. Next thing Margate would be asking for his money back and Luke could ill afford that at the moment. The local authorities didn't exactly condone his activities, but they turned a blind eye if he made the appropriate 'considerations.' Carlin's World was becoming one of the few places left where people could hunt, and even here, it was becoming harder with each passing season. There ought to be a better way to make a living.

When at last they reached the campsite, Margate's humor had improved none. It was going to be a long few days.

oOo

Morning light saw the touch of rose and gold across the red-hued grasslands, and it saw Margate's mood hardly improved.

"Did you sleep well, Mister Margate?" asked Luke as the man emerged from his tent.

"No. It was too hot." He scratched at his neck and yawned. "And something's given me a rash. Kept me up half the night."

"I'm sorry to hear that. Well, there's some coffee there."

Margate grunted and moved to help himself. As he passed, Luke caught a whiff of something sweet like cologne. Strange for a man to wear cologne out here, but to each his own. While Margate sat and sipped at his coffee, Luke busied himself stowing gear in the ATV. He'd had the vehicle painted in black and white zebra stripes — the clients seemed to like that. The solar-powered vehicle also gave more of the frontier illusion — two men alone against the wilderness.

By the time full light had arrived, tingeing the

sky with pale greenish blue, Luke was just about ready. Margate was propped on one of the foldaway chairs, scratching at his shoulder and muttering. Luke stooped to retrieve Margate's carelessly discarded mug, rinsed it, shook it out and stowed it with the rest of the gear. He looked down at the man with distaste.

"If we're ready, Mister Margate?"

"I suppose so. I don't mind telling you, if you don't come up with the goods soon, you're not the only one who's going to hear about it. If you don’t start delivering, you won't get another client when I'm done. I'll see to it."

"All right, Mister Margate. I'm certain we'll find what you're after soon. Just be a little patient."

"Patient! I learned a long time ago just how far patience gets you." He pushed himself to his feet and made for the vehicle, leaving Luke to fold away the chairs and stow them. By the time Luke climbed up in the driver's seat, Margate was drumming on the doorframe with his fingers. "Well, are we getting under way or are we going to spend all day sitting here looking at your scenery?"

"Yes, Mister Margate. Just sit back and enjoy the view. We've a pretty long drive ahead of us."

"Humph. About time. And when we get there, you can find something for this damnable itch." Margate was scratching at his thigh now, his big red face looking even redder. If he went on like this, he’d burst a blood vessel before the day was out.

Luke kicked the motor over, thankful for the growl of the engine noise to cover Margate's complaints. The man was still scratching and the sweet cloying odor of his cologne filled the cab. Luke knew both were going to get worse as the day wore on and the cab grew steadily hotter. Inwardly he sighed, not looking forward to the journey ahead.

oOo

By the time they reached the next campsite, Margate was no better. He scratched persistently at varying locations on his body and cursing under his breath. Luke pulled into the campsite and killed the engine.

"I put this down to you, McEvoy."

"Look, Mister Margate, it's probably just an allergy. You've come into contact with something you're allergic to, that's all. I'll check the med kit once we've set up the camp. There's bound to be something in there that'll ease your discomfort."

"Look at this!" Margate thrust his arm under Luke's nose. Large red bumps covered the skin, angry and raw from all the scratching. A waft of sweetness washed over Luke's face.

"It looks like an allergic reaction to me," said Luke. I'm bound to have some antihistamine cream in the med kit. Um, Mister Margate, if you don't mind me asking...what cologne do you wear?"

"Cologne? What the hell are you talking about?"

"That smell. Sort of sweet?"

"I don't smell anything. Stop trying to change the subject. It won't do you any good."

Luke frowned as Margate clambered from the vehicle and slammed the door.

There was one consolation. There had been plenty of signs of veldt bulls on the way in. The sooner they could bag a couple and get out of there, the sooner he'd be rid of Margate. He only hoped the man hadn't caught anything. They were at least two days from a relay station and professional help if Margate really was sick. He'd deal with that possibility later. He lowered himself from the cab and with a quick glance at Margate, set about unloading. Margate simply propped himself on the side of the vehicle and watched.

"Mister Margate, the sooner we get this stuff unloaded, the sooner I can look for that stuff for you."

"Well, you'd better stop flapping your jaw and get on with it."

Luke narrowed his eyes and did just that without saying another word. Finally, he dug out the med kit and located the cream. Margate snatched the tube from his hand, which was just as well. The smell from the man was becoming overpowering. Luke left him to it and set about starting a fire. A slight breeze ruffled the tent flaps and gently stirred the flames. He peered off through the fading light, across the red-grassed plain and felt a brief sense of contentment. He could almost forget that he was not alone. This is what had drawn him to this place — the unspoiled beauty and the solitude. But the illusion was quickly shattered. Margate stalked across and tossed the tube at Luke's feet.

"That seems to have done something, but the damn rash is still there. First, you take me on a wild goose chase. Then you drag me through the heat with lumps breaking out all over my body. Allergy! Like hell. I bet it was that 'harmless' creature of yours."

As if on cue, a low keening sound broke out over the grasslands — from more than one direction.

"There you go!" said Margate waving his arm. "More of the damn things."

Luke sighed. "I assure you, they're harmless. Look, why don't you sit and enjoy the view while I fix us something to eat. There's nothing quite like twilight over the veldt."

"Listen, McEvoy, I've got no use for your views. If I wanted that, I would have brought a camera and gone somewhere civilized. I came here to hunt and we've done damn all of that. My patience is wearing pretty thin. You'd better come up with some results in the morning or you'll have some real trouble on your hands."

Luke bit back his reply, clamped his jaw shut and started preparing their evening meal. It gave him an excuse to stay far enough away from the man not to want to lash out at him and far enough that the stink of him didn't invade his senses.

And it wasn't just the physical stink — that sweet, cloying cologne-like scent. It was the stink of his attitude and his arrogance. For six seasons, he'd seen a succession of men like Margate and now, finally, it was beginning to wear thin. He picked at his food in silence while Margate shoveled at his without even a word of thanks. Luke stared out over the darkened plain, wondering what the hell had brought him to this.

oOo

The slither hound turned, snuffing. Something new filled the air — a sweet indefinable urge. He knew the taste, the sense of it. He turned to face the direction where he'd last caught the tang of ungulate, but there was nothing. Confused by this, he turned and sought. Another scent wafted over the grasses and with it came the smell he sought. Trembling, he shifted position. A low, deep sound grew in his throat, and he lifted his face to the sky.

An answering call came from beyond a small rise and another from a short distance away. The scent was driving him now, stirring within him. It was his. He would be the first. He had to be.

oOo

The keening of the slither hounds grew as the evening wore on. The breeze had lifted and the fire fluttered and danced. With every new call, Margate started in his chair and looked around nervously. The calls were definitely getting closer and they were deeper, different to the noise Luke was used to.

A call came from behind them, not twenty paces away. Margate shot to his feet, scratching at one arm and peering into the darkness. "I thought you said they were harmless, McEvoy. What are they doing?"

"I don't know. I've never seen anything like this before."

The grass stalks shifted around them and the sound of rustling came from not only behind them, but also from the opposite side of the fire. A slither hound called again, and its cry was answered from a spot from where movement had stirred the grass before. Suddenly, a slither hound burst from the clumped grass behind them and shot across the clearing. It was halfway across the circle when another burst from the grass on the opposite side and rushed to meet it. Both animals rose on their hind sections and, snapping and snarling, launched themselves across the intervening space.

Margate blanched and stumbled backwards, away from the furious conflict. Luke stood slowly, fascinated by what he was witnessing. It looked like a territorial conflict, but it was like nothing he'd ever seen before from the normally placid creatures. Further cries floated above the low veldt and were answered one after the other.

The furious combat was over in seconds. The vanquished slithered off into the long grass. The victor lifted its head, snuffing the air. It shifted its body and appeared to be dazzled for a moment by the firelight. It shifted its body again, regaining focus. It fixed its gaze on Margate and sniffed at the air again.

"W-what's it doing?" said Margate. "Get the rifle."

"Just stay perfectly still, Mister Margate," Luke told him quietly.

The slither hound shot across the campsite, straight at Margate and launched itself. A low vibrating cry came from somewhere deep inside it. The creature was on him before either man could react.

Margate cried out, then screamed. "Get it off me! Get it off me!"

Margate had fallen back, the hound fixed to one leg. It shifted position again, covering one arm, then planted itself on the big man's chest. Margate cried out with each new position, barely a pause between sounds. The slither hound was moving so quickly.

Then, just as quickly, it was gone, sliding off into the darkness. Damn they moved fast. Margate lay on the ground, groaning, rocking from side to side and clutching at his chest.

"It bit me," he groaned. "The damn thing bit me."

More sounds came from all around them. Luke scanned the surrounding area nervously. He had to do something and quickly.

Stooping, he lifted Margate to his feet, straining with the man's bulk. Draping Margate's arm over his shoulder, he half carried him to the vehicle, and pushing him bodily inside. He slammed the door, crossed to the other side and clambered in himself. The cries were coming from all around them now.

"Here, let me see," he said to Margate.

"Arghh, it hurts," Margate said through gritted teeth and held out his arm. Three large puncture wounds seeped blood, red and angry circles surrounding them.

"These aren't bites. They look more like some sort of sting."

"I don't care what the hell they look like. Do something!" He still held his other hand clutched to the place on his chest. From all around them came the cries of the slither hounds and they were getting closer. Margate leaned back against the door, his face screwed up in pain.

Luke shuffled around for the med kit, but he already knew there was nothing appropriate inside it and he had nothing more than simple first aid training. He had some painkillers and antiseptic. That would do for the moment, but he'd have to get Margate to the colony hospital. He only hoped the wounds hadn't been injected with some sort of venom.

"Do something," Margate breathed.

Luke shook his head and set about cleaning the wounds. He slapped on an analgesic patch, then, having second thoughts, slapped on another for good measure. He kept glancing out the window, checking that no more of the slither hounds were in range. As he touched the area around the wounds, Margate sucked in his breath and gritted his teeth.

"You'll pay for this, McEvoy," he hissed. "...pay for this."

Margate's eyelids fluttered, and his features slowly lost the rictus of pain. It was far too soon for the analgesics to have kicked in. Luke bit his lip. If Margate <u>had</u> been poisoned, then he was in real trouble. Checking that he'd seen to all the wounds, he shifted Margate's legs and made sure that the man's bulk was propped securely in the corner of the cab. He could leave their gear. There was no way he was going outside again. The important thing was to get Margate to effective help, and soon. He kicked the engine into life and glanced across at his client. The man's head was lolling on his chest.

Luke cursed once, and gritting his teeth, accelerated out of the campsite.

oOo

The trip back was hell. He had to stop every couple of hours to check Margate's wounds and with each stop, the inflammation appeared to become worse. The area surrounding each puncture was red and swollen, clearly uncomfortable. At least Margate no longer appeared to be in pain. He opened his eyes from time to time and looked blearily across the passing grassland while mumbling to himself, his expression glassy. Whatever was in the wound was acting like some sort of soporific. Occasionally, he dabbed at Margate's forehead with a moist cloth. Luke kept glancing at the man, seeing his livelihood crashing down around his ears.

It took nearly two days continuous driving for them to reach transmitter range. The emergency copter was with them in under two hours. They whisked Margate away, getting a full account of events on the way.

They landed at the base and whisked Margate away, with Luke looking on nervously.

oOo

Three days later, he sat in Alan Jackson's office, waiting to be pilloried. Jackson was the local official and the prime authority in the region. Luke didn't have long to wait.

Jackson stepped into the room and nodded to him, a grim expression on his face.

"Luke. How are you?"

"I'm fine. I'm more worried about Margate."

Jackson's expression eased a touch. "Oh, he's fine too. He's already taken off. Once they'd removed what was in those wounds, he was just fine." He waved a hand dismissively.

Jackson propped himself on the edge of his desk, supporting himself with his hands behind him. He looked as if he was waiting for something.

Luke knew why he was here. This was it. "I'm sure he had a few things to say, though."

"Oh, Margate was screaming legal action from one side of the system to the other, but when we told him he'd effectively been laid by one of the local fauna, he shut up pretty quickly."

Luke paused. "I'm not sure I understand."

"He unknowingly found himself a part of the slither hound's reproductive cycle. The slither hound that attacked him was male. Only it wasn't an attack. The first contact, the first one that jumped on him, it must have been a female. The doctors found traces of spore all over Margate's clothes. It was pretty easy to work out what happened. The spore causes an itching reaction, the subject scratches and opens the skin enabling the spore to burrow into the flesh. The host transports it to another location where the male slither hound then fertilizes it. The scent that's produced acts as an attractant. The male slither hound doesn't have a sting. What it's got is a reproductive organ. In effect, we told Margate he'd been humped by Carlin's World's variant of a dog. We threatened to publicize the fact wherever we could." Jackson grinned.

Luke's head was suddenly full of the picture of an old Aunt that the family dog had taken a shine to. Every time she visited, the family dog had wrapped its forelegs around the reluctant woman's legs and pumped away as she step-slid around the house, trying to ignore it. It didn't help that the slither hound looked so much like a Cocker Spaniel. He laughed aloud. "I would really have liked to see the look on his face when you told him."

"But," said Jackson, becoming more serious, "it brings up another issue. Your little hunting activities are the reason this occurred in the first place. We presume that the veldt bull acts as the normal host for transport of the spore. We've had reports of some recent seismic activity near the area where you first made camp. Seems it coincided with the slither hound's breeding cycle. It only happens once every few years. It would explain the scarcity of veldt bulls in the area and the need for the slither hound to find a substitute. Margate just happened to be the candidate."

Luke nodded thoughtfully. "Yes, I can see that making sense."

"But I'm afraid we're going to have to call a halt to those hunting expeditions. It has clearly become dangerous and if it has a chance of disrupting the local fauna's life cycle, we can't afford to turn a blind eye. But, more importantly, if it gets out that there's a threat to people, it's going to damage our potential as a colony world."

This was it. Luke had known what was coming and he'd already been thinking hard. "Listen, Alan. I was getting a little tired of it anyway – tired of the animals. I mean animals like Margate, not the local sort."

Jackson nodded. "So what's your alternative?"

Luke considered for a moment, framing the words for the idea that had been running through his mind. He'd already had nearly three days to think about it. "You know it's a beautiful planet – unspoiled, and I've been thinking. There's more than one way to bring in a few bucks. I might need your help, but I think we're well enough established out here now to be more than an outpost colony world. I'm sure there's someone out there that'd pay to get away from the rat race back home. Why pander to those who would spoil the place anyway? If what you say about the slither hounds is true, give it a bit of time for the veldt bull population to become re-established, and it'll be safe to take people out there again, won't it? But this time, we wouldn't even have to let them out of the vehicle. Take them out there with recorders instead of rifles this time. It may take some time, but I could set up some sort of lodge out there."

Jackson smiled and nodded. "It *will* take some time."

"I know, but I think I know enough about the place by now to be able to do it. And there'd be work for others out there if they wanted in. We don't really want to become an established part of an alien breeding cycle, now do we? But it's funny how Nature will have its way."

-The End-

Negative Density

Stars spattered the velvet black through the viewscreen, points between infinities. Normal space. But there were too many abnormalities in normal space. Peterson turned his flight couch away from the view and sighed. He hated these solo runs in the newer surface-to-space ships. He guessed they had to include a viewing screen in them, but it made him feel no better. All that distance, all that space—it made him small and aware of his own tiny place in the scheme of things. He preferred the older ships; the type where he had to take a shuttle up to orbit and he didn't have to look at the outside if he didn't want to. Surrounded by banks of instruments, he was secure, his space defined. Here, his boundaries were displaced by a vision of infinity and if he stared at it long enough, he could almost feel himself falling.

Then there was the drive, sitting just below his field of vision, bulging like some weird growth from the ship's nose. It took some getting used to.

They'd taken long enough to believe the Alcubierre Drive was safe enough inside the atmosphere. The advances in exotic matter containment had finally gained enough acceptance to let long-haul trading become a reality with the reduced costs of surface take-off. Miguel Alcubierre had a lot to answer for. But that was years ago. It had been forty years since his first speculative paper back in 1994.

Peterson leaned over and tapped up the inventory—sixteen crates of exotics. Vegetation. Just what he wanted. On the long haul, there was nothing to occupy him with the cargo; it looked after itself. The crates were sealed and had their own portable environment units. He thought he might as well check them out all the same. There was at least an hour until jump, and it was better if he kept his mind busy. He didn't want to think about what would be displayed on the viewscreen when the drive kicked in—he'd seen it too many times before, and every time it was different. If he told anyone about the things he saw out there, he'd be off ship work quicker than he could blink. He could hear it now. "Peterson's finally lost it." They'd 'tut' and shake their heads, and he'd wind up posted to some warehouse job planetside. There was a whole bunch of spacer's folklore about what the drive did to your brain, and he had no intention of being the next victim.

With the ship set on auto and Verdi pumping through the com system, he wandered back to the cargo bay to check on the crates. Perhaps he ought to think about listening to something else leading up to the jump—something lighter.

He leaned against the first crate while he looked down the even line. High-strength webbing ran from ceiling to floor holding the large metal containers in place. Monitors on the front of each crate glowed green, showing the environment was at optimum. He strolled down one side, tapping the walls of each storage unit as he went. So much trouble for a collection of houseplants; it hardly seemed worth it. This was where advances in technology got you—a high-cost courier service for the mega-rich.

He crouched down so he could see through the small rectangular window on the front of the last crate and peered in at his cargo. Deep purple leaves tapered to sharp spines at the end. In the centre of each sat a globular fleshy flower, oozing some sort of clear sticky liquid. Peterson thought they were ugly, but each to their own. There was no accounting for taste.

He hummed along to the soundtrack as he walked up the other side. No, the opera would stay. It was too much a part of the routine. Stretching across to grasp a thick strand of webbing in each hand, he leaned his weight back against it and pulled. It seemed secure enough, so he tried the next one. It didn't hurt to double check. Happy that nothing was going to shift around, he gave the cargo bay one last look, then wandered back up to the flight deck.

Easing himself into the flight couch, he spun it away from the viewscreen. No point in making it worse until he had to look. He keyed off the music and sat waiting. Ten minutes to jump.

The last person who'd said anything about what they'd seen in that indefinable place that was jump space was Andy Scarborough. Scarborough had been a good pilot, but Scarborough was just a good pilot with a desk job now. The company wouldn't let him anywhere near a ship. No way Jack Peterson was going to let that happen. He was a pilot, and he was going to stay a pilot. The solitude of the haulage runs suited him just fine. All he needed was to raise enough capital to get his own ship, then he'd be free. No more company regulations to adhere to. Nobody to answer to but himself. There'd be a bit of work in building up the business initially, but once he was freelance....

The navigation unit chimed, telling him they were

approaching jump. Peterson scanned the readouts to either side and spun the couch around to face front. The squirming hollow deep in his belly had started. He swallowed and watched, waiting for the transition.

There, at the edges of the viewscreen, it had begun. The stars flowed together, smearing towards the centre. They dribbled inwards, picked up others along the way like drops of water and formed rivulets of pale light. Any moment and the jump drive would kick in. The containment field was lessening, channelling the forces that squeezed and warped the space in front of the ship. He felt the thrum of the changes through the couch and swallowed again. He could just imagine the vast blossoming behind him as space expanded to thrust the ship and all it contained forward.

Then the drive kicked in. The field imploded, sucking the traceries into a central globe that expanded as soon as it had formed, sweeping outwards across his field of view. Peterson gripped the arms of his couch, his fingers digging hard into the cushioned fabric. The ship was in jump space now—the space between reality. He was nowhere, and the writhing shapes and non-shapes in front confirmed that knowledge. There was no sensation of movement. He was sitting still, and the universe flowed around him. He didn't even want to think about what might happen if the containment ever failed.

He leaned forward in a futile attempt to find a pattern in the shapes, trying to ignore the warped bulge thrusting out from the ship's front. Every time it was the same thing. The starburst forms curled in and out of his perception like white noise on a vid screen, but none formed a sequence he could name.

Peterson had no idea how long he sat staring. He lost all sense of time in jump —if there was such a thing as time. His vision was starting to blur from staring too long when something snagged his attention. Then a shape coalesced in the corner of his vision. Tiny at first, it grew rapidly larger. He bit his lower lip as his mind went cold. He'd seen that shape before.

The image expanded to an all-too-familiar form in the middle of the random nothingness, and he gripped the arms of his couch still tighter. It was too familiar. His heart pounded and the noise of a growing fear rushed inside his ears. And there it was. He was looking out at a ship where no ship could be. The long, narrow shape with the bulbous protrusion like a massively deformed chin grew slowly in the field of blank and swirling light.

He was so bound in the vision that he almost missed the small indicator flashing to his left. Inbound communication. His heart skipped a beat. This was something new. There was no way it could be possible— not here in jump. Hesitantly, he reached out then withdrew his hand. Then slowly, slowly, he reached out again. A voice swelled through the channel.

"John...John Peterson. Listen to me. I know you can hear me."

He gasped. The voice, though distorted, was familiar.

"John, respond please. This is important. Forget about what you're feeling. There's nothing to be afraid of. Respond. You really are hearing this. Let me know you can hear me."

"Y-yes. I can hear you," Peterson said a little too loudly.

"Good, John. Now listen. It's important that you—"

"Wh-who are you?" he whispered at the communicator. Perhaps he *had* lost it after all.

"Just listen and pull yourself together. You've got to lose your cargo —jettison it. I don't care how you do it, just make sure it gets done before you make it planetside. Preferably drop it somewhere well out of reach."

Peterson shook his head. This was crazy. "I can't do that."

"John, forget about it. The amount of money you'll make isn't worth it. Do you want the chance to go solo? To have your own ship? Then listen to me."

Peterson buried his face in his hands. This could not be happening. When he looked up again the ship would be gone and so would the voice.

"John...? Can you still hear me? We haven't got much time." Then a wry laugh. "As if we've got any time, here."

Peterson swallowed and cleared his throat. "Yes, I can still hear you."

"Good, then listen carefully. The plants you're carrying —you have to get rid of them. That secretion round the bud indicates they're on the verge of opening. When they open, they will release something nasty —a viral entity. If the plants get to their destination, that entity will spread, and it's going to have a devastating effect. Do you understand me?"

"What effect? How come nobody knows about this?"

"Nobody knows about it because the things have

such a long gestation period. Nobody's seen these plants in flower before. We've just been finding too many new things over the last couple of years. How could anyone know they aren't safe? Think about it. Who do you think's going to get the blame when it happens...and what then?"

"How do I know I can trust you? How do I know I'm not imagining all this?"

"You're not. I know you don't believe this is happening now, but you'll review the logs later and you'll know I'm telling the truth. If you can't trust yourself, then who can you...?"

The voice was gone. The hiss of an open channel filled its place. Peterson lifted his face and looked at the viewscreen. The other ship was gone too. He shook his head and switched off the com.

He sank back in to his couch, watching the squirming shapes that echoed the feeling in his belly. Damned drive was finally starting to screw with his brain.

oOo

Peterson re-entered normal space and tried to find something to shake off the after-effects of his experience. He took a stroll down to the cargo bay and looked at the crates. They all seemed secure. One by one, he went to the small slit window in each and looked through, checking for any sign. The plants were just as he'd seen them before jump, ugly, but perfectly innocuous. The large fleshy globes continued dripping the pale fluid, and they did look strangely tumescent, but he saw nothing sinister. Each crate gave exactly the same picture. Peterson rubbed the back of his neck.

Maybe his subconscious mind had been trying to warn him about something. It had been like a lucid dream—sort of—a waking hallucination.

Somehow, staring at the visual white noise of jump space must have put him into a trance where he'd imagined the conversation. It was just some delusion triggered by his inner fear of the jump itself. There was no way anybody outside the company could have known about the cargo, nor the current state of it. Nobody at all could know about the condition of the plants except for himself. Well, there was only one way to verify it —get back on the ground, unload his cargo and he could review the tapes. He had another three hours before approach. Plenty of time to immerse himself in a book, listen to some music and try to put the whole thing out of his mind.

He walked slowly back up to the flight deck and flopped into the couch, determined to do just that. He keyed up a book, put on some music for background noise—Puccini this time—and spun the couch away from the viewscreen before putting his heels up. He tried to read for the next three hours, but the experience of the last relative hour or so made it hard to concentrate. Images of the phantom ship kept floating in his head, and the voice kept running over and over, telling him to dump the cargo. When the navigation console finally signalled approach, he felt relief. He watched as the visual field formed itself back into recognisable pinpricks, stars, and constellations—things he could put a name to. And hanging there, solid as the reality it represented, lay Home.

The instruments would handle most of the atmospheric manoeuvring, but as he approached, he opened a channel to the company field all the same.

"Incoming, Phil," he said, knowing the shift rosters off by heart.

"Hey, Jack. Is that you?"

"Yep. Should be down in around forty-five."

"Do my ears deceive me, or have you got that damned music of yours turned off for once?" The normality of Phil's voice brought him quickly back to reality.

"Each to their own, Phil. Each to their own. I'll see you groundside after we've got this stuff off-loaded," he said with a chuckle. "And you can buy me a drink for that last crack." He felt a lot easier now. He could almost forget the shakiness. Perhaps he'd just been working too hard. Building up a huge credit balance wasn't worth anything if he wrecked himself in the process.

"Deal," said Phil.

Peterson closed the channel and sat back. Something bothered him about the conversation, and he couldn't quite work out what.

oOo

He met Phil after they'd unloaded, and they went for the obligatory drink. He didn't tell Phil about the other ship. He didn't tell him about the message. He didn't tell anyone.

Scanning the logs had told him nothing. He'd listened to the voice over and over. Through the distortion of the com channel, it was hard to put a person to the voice, but at least the logs had told him that he hadn't imagined it. Knowing he wasn't Jack Peterson, madman, was some small relief. Life went on as normal.

He was nearing the end of his three-day lay over and he'd had time enough to get over his fears. He was looking forward to getting back to work. He had another run scheduled for exotics, and it would be good to get back out on the ship and busy, away from the space and time to think about what had happened on the last run.

He flipped on the news.

He was listening with half an ear when a name snagged his attention and he leaned forward. President Tanaka of the Combined Japanese Alliance had died during the night along with his entire household. The cause was unknown at present, but early indicators suggested they had all contracted a new fast-acting and deadly virus. Hospital workers involved in the case had also been struck by the disease and the whole area was under quarantine. Terrorist involvement was not being discounted. So far no group had claimed responsibility.

In a similar incident, closer to home, the leading industrialist George Margate, Chairman of Meta-Fusion, had been struck down along with all members of the Board of his company. All families and medical staff associated with the incident were undergoing observation and were effectively under quarantine. Analysts were trying to establish any link between the Margate and Tanaka incidents. If it was the work of an extremist group, use of biological weaponry represented a new and chilling phase to global terrorism.

The news report went into further detail, but

Peterson only listened with half an ear. He sat back in his chair and whistled. He was sure both names had been on his manifest. It could just be coincidence, but he was starting to have doubts.

The next morning, he flicked on the news again. More outbreaks of the mystery disease had occurred in the last few hours. Two more leading names in politics and industry had died during the night. Authorities were treating the incidents with the utmost gravity. The number of dead in the Tanaka incident had now reached fifty, and the figure was expected to grow.

Peterson placed his mug down carefully on the sink. A cold sensation was growing in the pit of his stomach. What had the logs said? What had the voice told him? Not bothering to listen to any more, he turned off the news and grabbed his keys. He had to get to the ship—he needed to check the manifest.

He called Phil on the way down to the field.

"Listen, Phil, just to let you know. I'm going aboard to check a couple of things."

"Jack? But you're not due to take off until tomorrow?

"Yeah, I know. There's just something I've got to check out. I'll explain it to you later. Okay?"

"Yep. It's your ship. Well, it's not, but it might as well be. You'll have your own baby soon enough. You free later? Want to go for a drink?"

"Yeah, maybe. I'll let you know."

He flashed his ID at the gates and drove straight over to the parking bay. Ten minutes later he was aboard, with the manifest keyed up in front of him. He leaned forward and ran his finger down the list.

Margate.

Tanaka.

Wilson.

Rogers.

Peterson licked dry lips and sat back in his couch. Every one of those names had appeared in the news reports. Every one of those names belonged to one of the victims. The list had other names on it, but somehow he had the feeling they'd be appearing on news reports too over the next few days. He read down the list again.

He turned to the communicator and cycled the logs. The familiar voice filled the flight deck.

"Good. The plants you're carrying —you have to get rid of them. That secretion round the bud indicates they're on the verge of opening. When they open, they will release something nasty —a viral entity. If the plants get to their destination, that entity will spread, and it's going to have a devastating effect. Do you understand me?"

He keyed it back and played it again. He turned and read down the manifest list, then he played it over.

"Jack, what are you up to in there? Are we on for this drink or what?"

It was Phil. "Jack? You up there?"

And then it struck him. The voice on the logs had called him John. Nobody called him John. He was Jack to everyone.

"Yeah, Phil. Give me a few minutes will you?"

He slumped back in the couch. This was crazy. He let the com log play on, listening to the voice and knowing there was only one person in the world that thought of him as John. Suddenly, what he had to do.

"... You'll review the logs later and you'll know I'm telling the truth. If you can't trust yourself, who can you...?"

He could be ready for take-off in about forty minutes if he moved fast. He wouldn't have to work out the co-ordinates. They were already in the navigator from the last jump.

If you can't trust yourself, who can you trust?

He flipped open the communication channel and paged the tower.

"Phil, listen it's Jack. I'm going to take her up."

"What? Have you gone crazy?"

"No, listen, trust me on this. I've got to take her up. Give me clearance will you."

"What's your route. What the hell are you doing?"

"I'll patch you through the co-ordinates once I'm airborne. There's too much to explain right now. You've got to trust me."

"How the hell am I supposed to trust you if I don't know what you're up to?"

"Just do it for me, Phil. I can't explain now."

"I'm going to get shot for this, Jack. You know that. You'll get us both shot."

"Look, I'll owe you big time on this one. Just do it for me will you? If you don't, I'm going to take her up anyway."

"Well, you'd better have a damned good explanation when you get back, pal..."

"Don't worry. I will"

If he ever got back...

He tapped the sequence for pre-launch and the ship awoke around him. He drummed on the edge of the communicator,

"Come on, Phil. Come on."

"Right. You've got clearance. Any time you're ready."

"Thanks, Phil. I owe you."

Peterson sat back in the couch and pressed the sequence to initiate launch. He hoped he was right about this. He wasn't thinking about the jump. That didn't matter anymore. Briefly, a memory drifted up from somewhere. A few years ago there'd been speculation about the effects of the drive, about the implications of space-time distortion that it might imply. He gave a wry smile at the thought. Maybe the speculations had been right; maybe they'd been wrong, but it didn't really matter anymore. He didn't care what shape it might be—all he needed was time.

-The End-

Fairy Lights

The first touch of their minds against mine made me shiver. I was alone then—I am still alone—but now I know why. I almost knew that first night, when Susan flew away.

That first day, our ship descended on Aurora, floating through the ruddy clouds, the attitude jets making the craft shudder and roar around us. Six of us sat in the descent vessel, the first base camp team. I was there as mission historian, to record and annotate for posterity, and I sat and watched the faces as I recorded. They glowed with excitement. Andy, Laura, Susan, Max, Ivan—all trained mission personnel. Then there was me. I was the outsider in the group, but then that was nothing new. I'd always been an outsider in one way or other.

The initial survey teams had decided the planet was safe. Things were different down there, but I'd been assured they would do me no harm and I believed them. The virgin world below beckoned with the promise of dreams to be fulfilled. For me, it was history in the making and that was enough. And almost being a part of it.

"So, Andy," I said. "How does it feel to be a pioneer?"

Andy grinned back at the camera lens and struggled for something to say.

"Well, I guess it's better than sex," he said. "Oh, hell. Can you cut that, Phil? I reckon I ought to say something meaningful, right?"

"Sure. Take your time."

Andy ran his palm back across his stubbled head, adjusted his seat then looked into the camera again. Square jawed and deeply tanned, he looked the part. His clear blue eyes fixed the lens with intensity.

"I feel proud," he said. "Proud to be among the first to take our dreams to the stars."

That brought a slow handclap from the rest of the crew.

"A bit thick isn't it, Andy?" said Laura. "Hey, guys, I think he might be after the Academy Award."

"And playing Andy Johansen is ... himself," said Max.

The others laughed and I joined in. The good-natured banter continued to the ground, Andy looking sheepish.

I planned to pipe the images up to the main ship at the end of every day, after I'd finished editing them. I thought perhaps I'd leave Andy's bit in.

As the ship touched down, the others were busy with their instruments and readings. I let them get on with it and sat back, slightly envious, recording it all. I'd often dreamed of being in their position but hadn't made the grade. I'd done the tests and the company physicals but failed on the first attempt. Historian was the next best thing. I wasn't really a member of the team but being there with them was about the next best thing.

Our landing vessel was big—big enough to accommodate all of us for an extended duration if we needed it—and as strong as a rock. It had been designed to withstand anything the planet could throw at us, but as we were there to set up the first *real* base on Aurora, secretly all of us hoped it wouldn't come to that.

It took an hour or so for them to finish the final checks before they were ready to open the doors and then, one by one, the crew stepped down to Aurora's surface. I followed, camera on my shoulder, capturing it all for the records. Together we looked out over hills and fields touched with crimson and breathed in the moment. Max whistled softly.

"Will you look at that," he said.

Susan knelt down and fingered the tightly clumped knobs of vegetation packed hard against the ground.

"It's like a miniature gorse or heather," she said, more to herself than anyone else. "You wouldn't want to walk barefoot on this stuff."

She got to her feet, brushed off her gloves and like the others, stood staring at the alien landscape stretched out before us.

"All right, all of you," said Andy finally. "We

could stand here looking at this all day, but we've got work to do. Max, Ivan, you start breaking out the prefabs. The rest of us can start lugging. We've got a lot of stuff to shift. You too, Phil."

Ivan stood looking at Andy with his hands on his hips. His thin face held a slight quirky grin. "Well, as official team driver, I say we ought to take a bit of a spin first," he said. "It'd be a shame to waste this light, now wouldn't it?"

Andy shook his head, all seriousness. "We don't break out the vehicle until we've got the camp set. You know the drill as well as I do, Ivan," he said.

"Yeah, okay," said Ivan reluctantly, then gave a shrug. He headed back inside the ship to start shifting the equipment.

The crew all got on pretty well, and technically had the same ranking, but when it came down to it, Andy was the one in charge.

"And you too, Phil. You waiting for anything in particular?" he said.

"Um, no ... sorry," I said and tore my gaze away from the gently rolling fields. I could have stood there for hours drinking in the strangeness, but I shook my head, took a deep breath of the slightly fragrant air and went inside to help.

It took us about five hours to get the makeshift camp into some sort of order. The prefab bubbles slotted into place perfectly and looked like strange, silver golf balls scattered around the ship. I captured it all for posterity—or at least company archives and promotion clips—during the short breaks between shifting.

As the Auroran evening drew in, we cracked a couple of bottles reserved just for the occasion, so staking our claim to the planet; we were going to make this new world our own. Andy finally relaxed, satisfied that we had done enough for the day. He'd been in touch with the mother ship from inside the lander while the rest of us stared out of the communal dome at the purple sunset.

"Okay, guys," he said as he joined us. "Hey, save me some of that."

"Well, I don't know whether we should," said Laura, her pale round face showing mock disapproval.

"Yeah, mission leader and all that," said Max, swinging the bottle out of Andy's reach. "Have to be in full command of your faculties."

"I'm surprised he's deigned to join us," said Susan, only half-joking.

"Come on, guys. Mission hat off. Sure, we can have a good time, but the company's paying us to do a job too. Be fair. We've got to be prepared for any eventuality, not that anything's likely to happen." He made an ineffectual grab for the bottle.

"So, what do you say?" said Max, dancing his stocky form out of reach. "Should I let him have some?" He held the bottle at arm's length, away from him.

Andy gave up trying to grab for the bottle and stood with his hands outstretched, pleadingly. Max finally relented and passed it over. Andy poured a cup and joined us over at the main window. The dome light spilled out into darkness; the only illumination on the vast undulating plane, but far above, flickers of lightning or something else showed within the clouds.

"A toast," said Andy. "To the first base team on Aurora."

"To us," we said and raised our glasses. We stood and watched the deepening night in silence after that. Over the rim of my glass, I thought I saw vague shapes shimmering in the distance, but I couldn't be sure. I dismissed it as the result of staring through my lens on and off most of the day. Then it came again, something swooping up toward the clouds above the distant fields.

"What the hell was that?" I muttered to myself.

"What is it, Phil?" asked Laura.

I peered into the darkness, but I couldn't see anything. The shape had gone.

"Oh nothing. Just tired I guess," I said.

I didn't want to say anything. I wasn't trained mission personnel after all, and I wanted to be sure I'd seen something. It was probably just my eyes, or perhaps the wine playing tricks on me. I stared at the clouds for a long time but saw nothing more.

Finally, we drifted to our individual bubbles.

I slept like a baby. The exercise of setting up the camp had worn me out. My sleep inside the bubble was painted with images and color. The vague shapes that had shimmered in the distance tiptoed through my dreams sprite-like. Every time I reached for them to give them shape, they retreated into the background. When I woke, they scurried away, almost forgotten, but they stayed lurking as a half memory in the back of my thoughts.

Normally, I wasn't much of a morning person, and I'd stagger around until I'd had my first caffeine shot, but this time it was different. I woke feeling light and airy, full of energy and eager to get on with the day's tasks. I bounced around the bubble in the slightly lighter gravity, dressing, collecting my gear, eager to join the others.

Most were already in the mess bubble by the time I arrived. I could feel the energy infusing the group as I entered. They seemed to have caught whatever was coursing through my own veins. I nodded to each of them and grabbed a ration pack for myself.

"Morning, Phil," Ivan said and grinned. "Almost the last. We're just waiting for Susan. What a great day, eh?"

And we kept waiting. After a time, Andy's expression darkened.

"Has anyone seen her?" he asked. "Laura? You want to go see what's happened to her?"

Laura nodded and ducked out. I tore open my ration pack and sat chewing, one hand resting on my camera. I wanted them all there so I could record the first breakfast on Aurora.

Laura reappeared a few minutes later. She poked her head around the door and leaned on the frame, her short dark hair framing the worry on her face.

"There's no sign of her. She's not in the bubble. I can't find her anywhere."

"Did you check the lander?" asked Max.

Laura nodded.

"Well, she can't just disappear," said Max. "Maybe she's in one of the other bubbles."

Laura shook her head and hung on the doorframe waiting for suggestions.

One by one, we turned to face Andy who cleared his throat.

"Yeah, well, as Max said, she can't just have disappeared. She's probably noticed something and gone off to investigate." He sounded unconvinced. "She knows the routine." He scratched his chin, then sighed. "I'm sorry guys, but we're going to have to find her."

Max groaned.

"Look, can't we finish breakfast first?" said Ivan. "She can't have gone far. And what's out there that could possibly harm her? Nothing."

"Come on, Ivan. You know how it is. By the book. Max, you're almost done. Why don't you go with Laura and see if you can find where she's got to? I don't want to make this official yet. Not unless we have to. Let's see if we can locate her and then we can forget it." He placed his hand flat on the table. "Although she sure as hell won't."

Max nodded, shoved the last of his breakfast ration into his wide mouth and walked out to join Laura.

"Great. Just what I need," said Andy with another sigh.

As I wasn't going to get the shots of breakfast I wanted, I made do with recording the remaining two. The whole thing was more subdued than I would have liked. I decided I could patch in other shots of them all together later.

After about a half-hour, Max and Laura returned.

"No sign of her anywhere," said Max.

"Great," said Andy. "This is cutting into our schedule. How could she do this? She knows the routine. Well, break out the vehicle and try tracking her by the signal chip. I hope to hell she's remembered to take the unit."

"Um, some bad news," said Laura. She held up Susan's unit.

"Wonderful!" said Andy. "What's got into her? Ivan, just do it. Get out the vehicle and find her, will you? There'll be hell to pay when she gets back."

Despite the seriousness, Ivan beamed. "Yes.

At last!" he breathed and slammed a fist into his hand.

"Listen, Andy," I said, wanting to do something. I didn't know why, but I thought I should be out there. "Can I go along? It'll give me an opportunity to get some good shots of the landscape, and I can at least feel useful."

"Well, I don't know...," he said, rubbing a hand across his stubble. "Yeah, okay. Why not? Without a signal, two pairs of eyes will be better than one."

"Right," I said to Ivan. "Give me a couple of minutes to get my equipment together, and I'll meet you alongside the lander."

Ivan nodded and went out to prepare. I joined him just as he was rolling the vehicle down from the ramp at the lander's back.

The vehicle was sort of like a four-wheel drive. Fat bubble tires gave it an all-terrain capability; not that it looked like we'd need it on Aurora's gentle fields. It was enclosed with thick roll bars forming a cage around the passenger area. There was room for four, but only the two of us were going. Ivan was grinning like a big kid when I clambered in beside him. All he needed was a helmet and driving gloves to complete the image.

"All set?" he asked.

I nodded. "Any idea which way we should go?"

"Not really. I thought we'd take a wide

circular sweep running in a spiral out from the camp. What do you think?"

"Sounds good to me."

Ivan accelerated out of the camp with a jolt that threw me back into my seat and slammed my lens into my eye-socket.

"Hey, take it easy!"

"Sorry," he said. "Just getting used to the controls."

"Yeah, sure," I said, knowing full well he'd spent years training in a vehicle just like this.

The vehicle bounced along, and I struggled to keep the camera steady. The smooth rolling plane stretched on, distance blurring the crimson ground cover into tones of mauve. There were no trees, at least not on this part of the planet. There didn't seem to be much in the way of life either—only the unbroken field of gorse, or heather, as Susan had called it. The thick purple clouds hung in a shadow above. I looked behind us and saw the twin tracks from the vehicle circling out from the campsite. I took a few shots of Ivan at the wheel, and he obligingly looked enthusiastic for the camera. Not that he needed me there for that.

We found Susan around midday. She was standing staring into the distance, her arms folded around herself. She didn't even notice as we drove up. Ivan idled the vehicle and opened his door. I had the camera going the whole time.

"Susan?" called Ivan.

She didn't respond. It was as if she didn't hear.

"Susan, what are you doing out here? Are you okay?"

Slowly she turned, a dreamy expression on her face. "What?"

"We've been worried about you. How could you just wander off like that?"

She lifted a hand to her brow and traced her fingers over the skin at her forehead. "It's just so ... I feel .... "

"Jesus, Susan. I don't know what you're on, but Andy's going to have a piece of you when we get back," said Ivan. She had turned away again and seemed to be watching something in the distance. She lifted her hands and rubbed at her shoulder blades.

"Susan, will you get in? I'm starting to get pissed," said Ivan.

She shook herself, walked over to the vehicle and stood staring up at him as if she didn't quite know who he was.

After a lengthy pause that made Ivan's frown grow deeper, she clambered up behind us. I turned to talk to her, but her eyes were focused somewhere in the middle distance. A slight smile played at the corners of her mouth. I turned back to face front as Ivan gunned the vehicle. Ivan's face was like thunder.

Susan said something, and I turned back to

look at her.

"Please keep off the grass," she said softly and giggled. She wasn't looking at us. She was staring up at the clouds.

At first, I didn't believe I'd heard right. She was smiling to herself. One hand still massaged her shoulder.

"What?" I asked. "Did you say something, Susan?"

Susan just shrugged and smiled, then turned from the clouds to watch the passing Auroran landscape. I looked at Ivan, but he just shook his head, hard lines etched into his face. Something was weird. Very weird.

We drove into camp and the others were arrayed waiting for us. Susan stepped serenely from the vehicle and walked over to join them as if nothing had happened. Andy's face radiated displeasure. The rest just looked bemused. Andy started in before Susan was ten paces away.

"What the hell do you think you are playing at, Susan? I expected a little more sense from you. What were you trying to do, jeopardize our mission?"

Susan merely shrugged.

At that moment, Ivan caught his foot climbing down from the vehicle and fell heavily to the ground.

"Ow! Dammit, this stuff's sharp," he said, picking himself up and looking down at his hands.

"You, okay?" asked Laura.

"Yeah, fine," said Ivan, picking a few scraps of vegetation from his gloves as he walked toward us. "Just stings a bit. It's gone right through the fabric." He rubbed his hands on his chest and joined the group.

Andy was still going at Susan, but it seemed to wash over her as if it meant nothing at all. The other team members cast concerned glances at each other.

Laura finally raised a placating hand.

"Listen, Andy, let's just cool down for a minute and work out what's happened here." As team medico, the group's welfare was Laura's prime responsibility.

Andy grudgingly stepped back and let Laura move forward to check Susan while the rest of us stood back and watched. She seemed to find nothing untoward. Despite repeated questions, Susan refused to be drawn about what had caused her to go off like that. Laura finally backed off with a concerned expression.

"I want her to get some rest. I'm sending her to bed for the rest of the day. There appears to be nothing physically wrong with her, but ... " She shrugged. "And Ivan, you let me take a look at those hands."

That night, Susan flew away.

We were gathered in the mess bubble, all tired from the final set up of survey equipment and the remaining camp prefabs. The lab was in place, and monitoring equipment. I'd got some good shots of the interplay between the team members during the day, and even managed to lend a hand here and there, so felt a little more like a part of the group. The feeling was good. It didn't happen too often.

We were sitting around a table, discussing plans for the next day, when Susan walked into the middle of the bubble. She stood looking at us, saying nothing, a faint smile on her face, her short reddish hair forming a nimbus in the dome light. Then she took off her shirt.

Max choked on his drink and came up spluttering. Laura stood and edged around the table toward her. Andy just sat open mouthed. Ivan snickered, and then stared, grinning from ear to ear. I don't remember exactly what I did, but I think I finally managed to close my mouth.

Before Laura had taken three steps, Susan held up her hand.

"No, Laura," she said. "Don't bother. It's not important. I'm fine. You'll see. You'll all see."

Then she unfurled her wings—vast gossamer wings iridescent with rainbow colors—walked calmly out the door and took off into the night.

A couple of us raced to the window and watched her soar up and out into the purpling sky. Like an idiot, I'd left my camera on the table. The silence dragged on and on. Finally, someone spoke.

It was Andy.

"What the...?"

"I don't know," said Laura. "I'm not sure I ... You all saw her, right?"

"Uh-huh," said Max, nodding his head and still goggling at the place where she'd stood.

"Did she just— "

"Fly," giggled Ivan.

"Like, she had— "

"Yeah, wings," said Ivan. This time he laughed.

"What the hell's going on here?" Andy slammed his hand down on the table. He looked from Max to Laura and around the other faces, but everyone merely shrugged or shook their heads. Andy stood and walked over to the window. He peered out into the darkness, shaking his head.

"Andy, what are we going to do?" asked Laura. Andy shrugged without turning. He was still shaking his head.

"Please keep off the grass," said Ivan.

Andy spun. "*What*?" He almost spat the word at Ivan.

Ivan shook his head and looked away. I gave him a hard look.

Ivan was staring down at his hands. He was smiling.

Andy stalked back over to the table. "Well, what the hell is that supposed to mean?"

"It was just something she said," I offered.

Andy growled, turned and strode outside. He started calling Susan's name—shouting at the night sky. Max and Laura went out to join him. Moments later their voices joined his.

I looked out the window, but there was no sign of anything up there in the purple clouds. I turned back and saw Ivan, still staring at his hands and smiling. He turned his face to the window and looked out at the sky. There was an expression like longing on his face. He reached back and rubbed his shoulders. We were alone in the bubble.

I came back to the table and stood looking down at him. After a moment I sat down opposite.

"Ivan," I said. "What did you mean?"

"Hmm?" He dragged his attention back from the window.

I had a suspicion, but I wanted to be sure. "Ivan, about the grass. What did you mean?"

He shook his head and smiled. He turned back to the window. His face bore the same serene expression I'd seen on Susan's face earlier.

"Talk to me, man! Tell me what you know." He kept smiling, a dreamy expression, and shook his head.

It looked like I wasn't going to get any sense out of him, so I went out to join the others. Between calling for Susan, we tried to work out what had happened, but all of us were as lost as each other, barely able to believe what we'd seen, despite the suspicion lurking deep in my mind. We called and searched well into the night, but we saw no further sign.

By morning, Ivan had gone too.

As soon as we found him missing, we fired up the vehicle and went out searching. Though we rumbled around and around the crimson fields in shifts for most of the day, we found nothing. Andy made his report in the afternoon. He locked himself away in the lander, clearly a worried man. He was in there for over an hour. When he returned, his face was grim.

"We're to continue searching, in shifts," he said. "If we've not found them by morning, we're taking off."

Laura looked horrified. "You mean we're just going to --"

"That's right. Leave them here. Those are the orders. What else can we do? Aurora will be put under quarantine until we work out what the hell's going on here."

Max went next. I knew he would when I saw him sitting outside his bubble fiddling with a piece of equipment on the ground. I was still recording, but none of the images would see the light of day. Not yet anyway. I got the pictures of his transformation later that night. I recorded the way the dreamy smile played over his lips. I smiled myself as he peeled the shirt from his stocky body. Then those massive, beautiful wings unfurled as he stepped outside and soared into the night sky. I tracked him until the speck faded among the clouds. Then I walked in and told the other two. They looked at each other with expressions of disbelief. When they came back in, the disbelief had changed to a sort of fear.

Andy and Laura were out searching. I was sitting in my bubble, playing back the images and getting them into some sort of order. Then Ivan's voice came to me in my silence, filtering through the corners of my perception.

Phil, can you hear me?

"Ivan?" I said to the bare walls.

If only you knew how beautiful it was.

"Ivan, where are you?"

You can join us, be with us. You can be one with us.

"Are the others there with you?"

We are all here, Max, Susan and the ... others. It's so beautiful. I always dreamed of flying. Didn't you have those dreams? It's so easy, Phil. Come and join us. You belong here.

"Who are you talking to?" Laura popped her head around the door, a worried expression on her face and Ivan's voice faded.

"No one," I said.

"But I heard voices. Are you all right, Phil?"

"Yeah, I'm fine. You must've just heard the equipment." I waved my hand at the decks. "I was playing back some of the recordings." That seemed to satisfy her. She walked right in to the bubble and sat on the end of my bunk.

"What are we going to do, Phil? We can't just leave them here. I can't talk to Andy. I just can't believe they want us to go without them."

"I don't think we've got any choice."

"Have you got any ideas about what's going on?"

"None at all," I said, comfortable with the lie for the moment. "I wish I did."

Laura bit her lip and nodded slowly. "Well, as long as you're okay," she said.

"Yeah, fine."

She stood and placed a hand upon my shoulder. Just for an instant, I thought about telling her, about sharing with her what I knew. But I pushed back the feeling. I knew now there was too much at stake.

She left and slowly I packed the equipment away.

We spent all night searching. Orders came through that we were to wear extra protection on top of our normal environment gear, so we suited up. The full suits were heavy and clumsy, and though we'd trained in them, I still couldn't get used to the lack of mobility. If only I could be like Ivan and the others. Despite the discomfort, the protective gloves suited my purposes. They gave me the opportunity to do what I needed to.

We spent all the next morning packing what we could get away in the time. The company didn't want to take too much of a loss, so wanted us to salvage whatever we could. Finally, in the late afternoon, all the gear was stowed. Neither Andy nor Laura looked happy about what we were about to do, but it wasn't our job. The company could sort out the rest. Andy did the final checks, then with a roar and a vibrating shudder lifted us off Aurora and to the waiting mother ship above.

I've already worked out how I'm going to do it. I used the hollow spaces inside my cameras and my recording decks. It was an easy matter to collect the seed heads, push them inside, then seal them away from view while the others were busy loading the gear. I think I made it look like I was checking the equipment ready for travel. Hopefully there'll be enough there to seed the planet, a new planet far away from Aurora. Hopefully the seeds will take. Somehow, I know they will.

As soon as I get home I'll start. First, I'll resign, citing the stress of the mission as the reason. I should have enough funds to last for a few months, to get me from one place to the next. I won't need money after that. All I'll have to do is to reach down and grasp the nettle myself. And when I've joined the rest, all of us, we'll all be together, apart from those few we left behind on Aurora. But I know within that they're happy too.

Finally, at last, I'll be where I belong. We all will.

-The End-

Fool's Luck

Ryan P. Dulwich frowned down at the slimline compad in front of him and cursed. He'd blown the damned codes again. He had just one more attempt. If he got the sequence wrong this time, he'd have no chance of getting through the door. He scanned the corridor quickly, and then leaned over to examine the copied plans just to make sure. They showed that he was in the correct place all right. He adjusted his breather where it was pinching his high-bridged nose and bent his thin frame back over the deck to start reworking the sequences. Brushing the stringy hair out of his eyes, he wiped his hands on his coveralls and started carefully keying the codes.

Dulwich was pretty good at what he did. Just because everything on *The Progenitor* was outmoded or falling apart, it didn't mean it was his fault. So, he was a maintenance technician. So what? What did they expect? Launch a ship like *The Progenitor*, fill it with about four million passengers, then leave it for about seventy years or so; things were bound to start going wrong, weren't they? In that sort of situation, you had to make the best of it, and that was precisely what he was doing.

He'd planned it all perfectly. That was what luck was all about, and he was making his own luck right now. The crash they'd had in the main systems couldn't have been better if he'd planned it himself. The failure had wiped out the main registry, and the crews on *The Progenitor* had been struggling to catalogue what was on board ever since. The plan was for three separate groups to open the various storerooms and take a detailed record of what they contained. Working from the upper decks down, the crews would catalogue as they went. Dulwich had been smart; he'd decided to conduct his own private survey, starting from the bottom. He knew he'd meet the other teams in the middle some time, but because he was a part of the official search detail, he should have fair warning.

All the same, he was starting to become nervous. His luck could only hold out for so long. Every time he opened a new door, a new tension rose in his guts. He knew that eventually someone would put two and two together. He sighed. No point worrying about it now. It would happen when it happened. Until then, he intended to stay lucky.

With the next attempt, the compad got the codes right and the door's locking mechanism ground into action. He smiled beneath the breather and shot a look up the passageway to check no one had seen. There was no one around anyway. Even if there had been, what could be more natural than a maintenance tech doing quick soft overrides on failing equipment?

He gave the passageway one last check, then slipped his compad into the top pocket of his beige coveralls and started manipulating the door. It clearly hadn't been opened for a while, and he had to use a little persuasion. Using the flat of his hands against the panel and pushing, he eventually managed to ease it far enough open to allow him access. He slipped inside, locked the door behind him, then stood blinking as the illumination panels hummed into life, bathing the storeroom with soft white light. Ranks of shelves and storage bays lined the walls, and all were full. He grinned.

Dulwich sauntered down the length of the room, humming as he went. The plans had been right. This store was huge, and it was full to the ceiling with all sorts of equipment.

All it took was a cursory glance to tell that some of the stuff would be useless. There were crates and shelves and storage bays all packed with bagged and sealed parts and supplies. He walked past one bay, and it held row upon row of old, yellow environment suits hanging in neat rows. He reached out to finger one sleeve and his hand came away covered in dust. He brushed it off with a grimace. You couldn't get away from the dust; it got into everything, and he didn't want to think about what caused it. Four million people tended to leave stuff behind.

A brief check told him there were some items he could probably shift without much trouble, but there was a lot of dross as well. He'd sort them out later, leave the stuff he couldn’t sell and just take what he needed, what was marketable. There was always somebody to spend a bit of credit on the extra items he 'acquired'. Three generations of travel took a toll. Satisfied he'd seen enough, he moved back to the door, killed the lights, and headed out to meet his main contact.

oOo

The *Horizons* bustled with weekend customers, and Dulwich had to push through to get to his usual table. Masters was already waiting for him. The engineer's florid, meaty face wore a scowl by way of greeting. Dulwich dropped into the nearest chair and nodded. Masters said something, but Dulwich failed to hear the breather-muffled words above the noise of background music and the evening crowd.

"Sorry?" Dulwich asked and leaned over to hear better.

"I asked you what you got for me, Dulwich. Come on ... give."

The Engineering Chief was a useful contact. He had friends, and he could shift the goods with minimal fuss. It didn't mean Dulwich had to like him. Masters was peering at him over the top of his breather, waiting for an answer. His bloodshot eyes looked even more feral when Dulwich couldn't see the rest of his face. The mask was like a clear plastic snout, protruding from beneath the fleshy brow.

"Look, I might have something promising at the moment, but I want to check a few things out. Give me a couple of days. I'll get back to you. I've got a feeling though, we could make ourselves a real killing." Masters narrowed his eyes. Dulwich ignored the look and continued. "Anyway, how are you guys doing with the air plant?"

"What do *you* think?" Masters spat back. "Plant's a damned antique. So are the tools we gotta work with. We've been on it for a month now since the bloody thing started going wrong. It's gonna take time, and time ain't something we've got a lot of. Why do you think we got these new regs? If we don't get something together soon, we're gonna have to shut down sections of the ship. After that... "

"Yeah? That bad huh? I know what you mean about the tools. Some of the stuff I have to use is just —"

Masters snorted and turned away.

Dulwich leaned back. The conversation was clearly over, and the less time he had to spend with Masters, the better. At least there was one good thing about the breathers; they cut out the need for small talk.

He pushed back his chair and stood. Masters pointed a fat finger at him and cocked his thumb, giving him a final nod. Dulwich nodded back, turned, and shouldered his way through the crowd.

He took a few moments watching as people passed between the stores and along the wide corridors in couples and small groups. After a quick look in either direction, he set off towards the transit station.

It was late enough for most corridors to be free of traffic and that suited him fine. He did some of his best work at night — nobody around to get in the way. He looked over the other passengers before boarding. They might only be people on their way home, but he liked to know with whom he shared his space.

The family left after only eight stops, the young couple at twenty. That left one more — the teacher. He took the opportunity to cast a sidelong glance in the old man's direction. There was nothing about his grey-headed fellow passenger to make him suspicious, but Dulwich felt uneasy all the same. It was unusual for one of the Professional Services team to have business so far down the lower decks.

The transit bounced to a stop and Dulwich pulled himself to his feet. He stepped out quickly, casting a furtive glance behind. His fellow passenger looked up and nodded at him pleasantly. Dulwich nodded back, then quickly picked up his pace and slipped hurriedly into the passageway from the landing bay. He pressed himself against a wall and waited, listening. The transit doors hissed shut, followed by the rush of compressed air as the vehicle left, then nothing. After a few moments, he felt himself relax. He pushed himself from the wall and headed up the corridor.

He had the code logged now, and once he got to the storeroom, opening the door was easy. He entered without putting his compad away and slipped inside. He pulled his breather off and let it dangle around his neck. It only got in the way when he was working, and there was nobody here to see.

He started in one corner near the door and worked his way down the length of one wall, taking notes as he went. A third of the way down the first wall, he stopped in front of a cupboard. It was no different from the others lining the long room. He looked at it long and hard, hesitated, then pulled the door open. As the light revealed what lay inside, he stepped back with his mouth open, his arms dropping loosely to his side. There, within, lay shelf after shelf stacked with cylindrical, orange tanks. Almost a thousand tanks lay inside, maybe more, and he knew without checking exactly what they were. They were the tanks that went with the environment suits he'd found earlier. He stepped forwards and rapped his knuckles on a couple, listening. They appeared to be full. One by one, he started counting, a grin spreading slowly across his face.

High-grade oxygen mix. Someone would pay good money for the stuff, wouldn't they? Breathing without a mask would be like a luxury, and luxury items earned good money. There was enough here to last a good few weeks. This was real luck. He could worry about the rest of the storeroom later. He stood thinking for a moment, chewing at his lower lip. He had to get hold of Masters and work out how they were going to shift it. He closed the cupboard door and patted it affectionately.

Slipping back outside, he keyed the locking sequence. Already, he was dreaming about what he was going to do with the extra credit.

A motion at the end of the passageway snapped him out of his reverie and injected cold into the pit of his stomach.

There was someone down here.

Dulwich pressed back against the wall. He snapped his compad shut and slipped it into his pocket, listening. Ten seconds. Twenty. There was no further movement from the archway beyond, but he knew he hadn't imagined it. With heart beating loudly in his ears, he started towards the intersection. If someone had seen him emerging from the storeroom, he'd have some explaining to do — and just when things were starting to go right, for once.

The passage merged with another at its end, and it was the only way back to the transit. He paused just before the intersection and listened again. Nothing but the whir and hum of the ship around him disturbed the silence. Perhaps he'd been imagining it after all. Taking a deep breath and letting it out again, he turned the corner and walked briskly towards the transit bay.

As he stepped out onto the boarding platform, his breath caught in his throat. Somebody *was* there. The

Professional Services guy stood on the end of the platform. He felt sure he'd left him in the transit.

The old man turned to look at Dulwich and his eyes grew wide. Puzzled, Dulwich returned the look and nodded, but the old man kept staring at him, a shocked expression on his face. It was obvious the old man knew what he'd been doing. What the hell was he going to do now? He glanced around the platform, lifted a hand to rub his chin. Then, with a start, he realized. He'd forgotten to replace the mask. With all the notices up everywhere, no wonder the guy looked at him like that. He scrabbled for the breather hanging around his neck and slipped it into place. Stupid. Here he was trying to maintain a low profile and what did he do? Stupid.

They stood forever on the platform, Dulwich avoiding the old man's looks. He boarded the transit as soon as it arrived. His heart still raced, and kept racing as the old man boarded with him and sat opposite. Fighting to appear calm, he kept his gaze fixed above the old man's head, refusing to meet his eyes.

The journey seemed to take an age, but finally the transit bounced to a stop. Dulwich waited for the doors to open and hastily headed out into the crowd. He resisted the urge to glance back over his shoulder, and tried to lose himself in the throngs. He couldn't tell without looking whether the old man had left the transit, and he couldn't risk a look backwards, not now. He cursed himself all the way to the *Horizons*.

Once inside the bar, he found his usual spot and sat nervously watching the door. The old man didn't show. No one showed. Dulwich concentrated on getting steadily drunk, still furtively watching the door as he sipped slowly beneath his mask.

oOo

It wasn't till the following evening that Masters turned up, and Dulwich had been nursing a drink for at least an hour by the time he did. Eagerly, he waved the beefy figure over to his table, filling with relief. The engineer already carried a drink, and he set it down on the table before pulling up a chair.

"Well?"

"I think I've got something, Masters. Got me a good source this time."

He didn't mention anything about his encounter on the transit.

"Mm-hmm. So tell."

"I've got hold of some ... oxygen mix." He whispered the last words and Masters had to lean forwards and strain to hear. Dulwich watched as the engineer narrowed his eyes and drew back. Dulwich waved him closer impatiently. "Look, I was thinking. You know, these masks are such a pain. People are going to pay good money for their own source of air, aren't they? They can open a bottle in their quarters, let it out on slow release, not have to worry about keeping the masks on. Air's so bad now you have to work at breathing. People'd pay for that wouldn't they? Pay to get these damned things off their faces. They could seal their vents and have their own private supply. What do you think?"

Masters looked thoughtful. "You might just have something, Dulwich. You've been putting that little brain of yours to work, haven't you?" He paused, looking at him with a calculating gaze. "So, how many of these things you got?"

"I tell you, there's hundreds of the things, maybe thousands. I don't know. Haven't done a full calculation yet, but there's plenty of them. Think you can shift them?"

Masters looked even more thoughtful, then grimaced beneath his mask.

"Gotta talk to a couple of people." He paused, thoughtfully, then seemed to come to a decision. "You wait here. I'll be back in a while."

The engineer slipped out and Dulwich sat and watched the crowd while he waited. He knew this was risky — if Professional Services found out, it would be a capital offence for sure.

He watched the crowd uneasily. People tilted their masks up to sip at their drinks through tubes, then quickly popped them back in place again. Nobody even glanced in his direction. Things had really changed over the past few weeks. Dulwich turned back to his own drink and stirred it with its tube.

A tap on his shoulder spun his head around with a start, but it was only Masters, standing over him. The engineer gestured at him to get up and follow. Negotiating his way through the people, he did as the engineer directed. Business was business. The burly engineer checked over his shoulder once or twice to make sure Dulwich hadn't lost him in the crowd, and headed off down a side corridor. Masters stopped halfway down the passage and stood waiting for him, then motioned him closer as he drew near.

"I just wanted somewhere we could talk freely."

"Okay, so talk."

"I've already been in touch with a couple of people, and I've generated some interest. You gonna show me the stuff?"

"Um, listen Masters, I don't think that's such a good idea. Maybe I'll just find my own sources. You know that's not how I work." A trace of unease wormed into his chest.

"It's not gonna hurt to show it to me. Just so's I can make sure of what you've got."

Dulwich shook his head.

"Fine. That's the way you want it." Masters raised one thick arm and waved towards the end of the passageway.

A large shadow suddenly loomed at the end of the corridor. He quickly turned and looked to the other end, but there was another figure blocking that avenue as well. Dulwich felt the chill as the silhouetted figures advanced towards him.

"Masters, what the hell are you doing?" he hissed. "We had an arrangement. You know you can't find the stuff. You need me."

"Mr. Dulwich, you're quite wrong. Engineer Masters has no further need of your services, and neither do we." The voice came from behind him, and he spun to face it.

The white coveralls of Professional Services confused him for a moment, until he focused on the speaker's face. The man he'd thought was a teacher from the transit now stood in front of him. Dulwich stared back.

"Who the hell are you?"

"It doesn't matter who I am, Mister Dulwich. Suffice it to say, I represent Ship's Security. You might be interested to know that we've been watching your activities for a number of weeks, monitoring your progress on the Central Information System."

"But how did you —?"

The old man raised his hand.

"That's not important. How stupid do you think we are, Mister Dulwich? We chose not to interfere in your activities at first. What you were doing suited our purposes quite nicely. You might as well have been working double shifts for us. But now, in the current crisis, we felt we couldn't let it continue, especially in light of your latest discovery. Masters has told us all about it. Its significance obviously didn't escape you. Well it didn't escape us either. Masters has been keeping us informed of your finds and we've been able to verify them as we went along. We did have a few problems accessing your personal lists at first. I have to give you credit for that." He motioned for the figures standing back at either end of the passageway to join them. "Now, Mister Dulwich, you're going to accompany us to the storeroom and use your codes to gain access. Then we'll see exactly what you've found."

"No! Not a chance!"

He shoved at the guy from Security and slipped past him, making a dash for the end of the corridor, but ran straight into a wall of muscle. They grabbed him by the arms and bundled him back. He struggled against their grip as they shepherded him towards the transit bay.

They descended in silence. The two security men flanked him, and the old man stood in front, with Masters behind. Dulwich's heart pounded in his ears, and he felt like his bladder was going to burst. Security had known all about him all along.

It seemed like an eternity before they arrived at the storeroom door. Dulwich keyed the sequence into his deck as they stood over him, almost fumbling the codes as his fingers failed to work. Finally, the lock ground open and Masters shoved at the door. The engineer entered first, pushing roughly past him. A firm hand on his shoulder propelled Dulwich into the room after him, and Ship's Security followed up behind.

It didn't take long for Masters to look up and down the rows of storage bins and shelves to assess what was there. He opened the cupboard containing the cylinders and nodded grimly to the security man.

"Yes, there's enough here to keep us going — for a while at least. Let's see what else we can find."

Dulwich leaned against a wall and watched, helpless. Suddenly Masters stopped in front of a large storage bin resting inside a deep alcove. He bent over it and reached in to retrieve something. He stayed there, bent over the bin for several seconds before he straightened, turned, and fixed Dulwich with an accusatory stare. His face was red with anger.

"You bloody fool!" Masters shouted at him. "You know what these are?" He ripped his mask off and threw it on the floor. "These," he said, hefting a large plas-sealed piece of machinery in one hand, "are the parts we need to fix the air plant! You just about did make a killing. All of us would have been dead within four months without these — you included, you stupid bastard."

Dulwich lowered his head and looked down at the floor. He swallowed, pulled his mask down, and let out a deep breath.

The older Security man stepped in front of him.

Dulwich looked up, knowing what was coming.

"Well, Mr. Dulwich, you were almost responsible for endangering the ship ... and you know what that means."

Dulwich nodded and swallowed again.

The old man stared at him with a stern gaze, drawing out the moment. "But it appears you have done us a service after all. Because of your 'extra work' and lucky for you I might add, it looks like we might just survive the current crisis. I think, for that reason, though every instinct tells me otherwise, so will you."

Dulwich looked across at Masters, then back to the Security Officer, and frowned. Slowly the realization dawned. They weren't going to space him after all. So what if they locked him up for a while?

He drew in a shaky breath of relief, and held it before slowly letting it out again. He closed his eyes, not even daring to let the smile that was building show on his face. It didn't matter what Masters thought of him. Ryan P. Dulwich really was a lucky guy. He'd soon find something else to do. After all, you made your own luck, didn't you?

-The End-

Raven's Eye

Iliana knew she was being watched. She couldn't quite tell from where, but that slight tightening between her shoulders alerted her. She let her hand stray towards the hilt of the small dagger at her waist, while she continued to poke at the remnants of the poorly made fire before her. The ashes were cold now, but she could still catch the smell of them over the scent of old pine needles that littered the small clearing where she crouched. There was a larger blade strapped slantwise across her back, the hilt extending above her right shoulder, but she didn't want to make any move toward it yet. Those she followed had left this clearing some time ago, but they could still be somewhere nearby, concealed within the surrounding trees.

Across the other side of the open space stood a bird, a large black, bird, its head cocked slightly to one side as if listening. Iliana narrowed her eyes at it, then glanced up at the sky. The light was starting to fade. Yet still she could not shake the feeling she was being observed. She flexed one shoulder, as if to shrug off the feeling, and glanced around the clearing edges, scanning the tall conifers for movement. The bird hopped a few steps, stopped, then tilted its head again. No, it couldn't be the bird, could it? But Iliana had heard of such things, of birds and other creatures being more than they seemed.

She reached for a small lump of fire-blackened wood and tossed it in the bird's direction. It flapped, rising briefly into the air, then settled, turning its head to peer at her, as if affronted.

"Well, what are *you* looking at?" she said.

Almost as if in response, it gave a rasping cry and took off into the air. It flapped around the clearing once, then disappeared among the treetops, leaving her alone with the noises of the forest. For a moment, she regretted her action. The bird had almost been company. Two days now, she had tracked through the hills, seeking her quarry with none but herself and the noises of the forest around her. She had seen signs of those she tracked, but that was hardly the same. Had it truly been two full days?

That afternoon, two days past, when she left the Old Mother's cottage, Iliana had been filled with anger. Now it had mellowed somewhat, but she still felt the desire to mete out some sort of proper punishment to the ruffians who had done what they had to the old woman. She could still see the image of the old woman lying on the floor, half in, half out of her doorway, her leg strangely twisted.

The Old Mother said there were three or four of them, as Iliana had helped her struggle from the floor, taking care of the injured leg, eased her old frame into a wooden chair and looked around at the belongings strewn from shelves and tables, tossed haphazardly across the bare earth floor. The smell of herbs and dried plants, of liquors and potions, was pungent in the confines of the small wooden dwelling.

"Listen to me, daughter," the old woman had said. "I will be all right. The leg is not so good, but it will heal. I 'm not really hurt so as it won't mend. But there is something more important. They took something from me — something they should not have. It was that which they came seeking."

Iliana had crouched in front of her, peering up at the time etched face, looking into those dark and knowing eyes with concern.

"What is it they took, Old Mother?" she asked.

"No, Iliana. I cannot tell you that. You must find the men who took it and bring it back. You will know it when you see it. It's a bundle wrapped in old red cloth and tied about with leather thongs."

That was strange enough. Though Iliana pressed her, the old woman would not tell her more of what the bundle contained, and though she had visited the old woman many times, she had never seen such a bundle, nor where the old woman might hide it. Rather, she was more concerned about her oft-time mentor. There was a large bruise starting to form on the Old Mother's forehead, a smear of dirt across her face, and Iliana had raised her hand, carefully pushing the strands of pale white hair away so she could see. The Old Mother gripped Iliana's wrist.

"No, I can see to that," she said. "It is what I do, after all. It 's more important that you attend to what you must." She released Iliana's wrist. "I knew this day would come. Go. Find them. Bring it back."

"But if you knew —?" said Iliana.

The old woman leaned forward and gripped Iliana's chin with one hand and leaned forward, fixing her with a stern gaze. "This is what you must do, child. Now go."

When Iliana stood, the Old Mother gave a satisfied nod, and then winced and frowned, the discomfort evident on her face. Iliana hesitated, but the old woman waved her away.

"Do as you must, child," she said. "But do it well. Do it as I know you can."

With those last words, she left the old woman sitting there, troubled to be doing so, her anger reaching up inside her, her jaw clenched tight. Whoever these men were, they would pay for what they had done.

The Old Mother had always been there, teaching, guiding, showing her things, ever since the times she first could remember. Iliana had never really known her birth mother. She had died when Iliana was barely three summers old. Instead, Iliana had grown up with her father, who taught her the ways of the forests, and how to use a blade and bow, how to track the signs on the forest floor and seek the paths in the more treacherous places. The Old Mother had tried to teach her about potions and the uses of various herbs and ingredients, but Iliana had shown more aptitude for other things, feeling more at home with a good strong hilt in her hand, rather than a collecting pouch. She was at home running between the trees or stalking silently, her bow held at the ready, the subtle scents and sounds of the forest all around her.

She missed her bow now. The fury that burned inside her had left her thoughts muddled. She had grabbed a few provisions, strapped on her sword, and taken off into the forest, not even thinking to leave word for her father. Later, when she realized, she knew that she could trust the Old Mother to give him word, but then she had no other thought driving her than to find the men who had done this thing.

She had little trouble determining which way they had gone. It was clear that they knew little of the forest, stumbling through the needles and small brush, leaving a clear trail. She had no idea how long ago they had left, but with such clear signs, she knew she would have little trouble tracking them down. Such hasty flight worried her. It was almost as if they had run in fear. Fear of what they had done? Fear of the Old Mother? No, that could not be possible. She was just an old woman living in the forest, after all.

But now, she could sense she was close to her quarry. Iliana played the events of that afternoon two days ago in her mind, as she sought a place to rest the night. She would start early in the morning, at first light. As she pushed a thick pile of dry needles together to make her bed, the picture of the old woman lying there kept returning to haunt her. They would pay for what they had done.

She heard the first sounds of them mid-morning. She was nearing the edge of the forest, the trees thinning and low scrubby bushes filling the spaces around their bases. The sound of voices drifted through the forest's edge, and Iliana slowed her pace. Picking her path carefully, she moved from tree to tree, keeping herself concealed as much as she could as she approached the forest's edge. She peered from behind a concealing branch, looking out on a sloping hillside, tufted grasses and the occasional bush breaking up the slightly uneven slope.

There were three of them, not four, sitting around the remains of a fire. She scanned the surrounding area, seeking a fourth, but there was no sign of any movement. It looked as if they were just now rising for the day, yet nearly a third of the day was already gone. She spotted a tree that would give her a better view, and carefully shifted her position, padding across the dry carpet of needles that cushioned the sound of her passage. This tree was closer, and the sound of their voices came to her more clearly. They were grumbling among themselves.

"Urghhh," said one. "My head hurts, and my mouth is like…"

"What do you expect?" said another. "You near finished all the wineskins yourself last night."

"Well, we deserved it, didn't we?" said the first. "We'll be home soon, and then we can celebrate proper."

The speaker was thick set, with matted dark hair hacked short about a square face. The other was thin, ratty faced with lank blond strands hanging around his dirty features. Iliana could not see the third one's face. His back was toward her.

"I don't like it, Haron," said Rat-Face. "We should have waited."

The third one spoke then, standing as he did so. He had long dark hair, tied behind his head, and he was tall. He busied himself with strapping a belt around his waist, in it, an ugly broadsword.

"Well, you can forget about that," he said. "We're far enough away from the old witch now. You worry too much. You'll feel different once we get paid."

Rat-Face spoke again. "Well, I still say you shouldn't have hit her."

The tall one laughed. There was something cruel and cold in the laugh, and Iliana felt the anger rising in her once again.

"You don't like it, Flit, you shouldn't be along." He turned, scanning the tree line, and Iliana shrank back. He had a dark, high-cheekboned face and even at this distance, she could see the scar running across one cheek and across his nose. He turned around.

"For all we know, the old witch is dead. She would be if you hadn't pulled me back," he said and laughed again.

Iliana ground her teeth and started reaching for her sword hilt. The other two were standing now, reaching for their packs and weapons. The man with the scar pushed Rat-Face and laughed again as his companion stumbled back and landed on his rump. Iliana stepped out from her hiding spot, determined to put an end to this right now. She was easing her sword out, striding forward, when a black flurry burst from the trees, right in her path, squawking and croaking up into her face. She stumbled back, hands in front of her face and quickly ducked into her place of concealment. Just as well she did, because the one with the scar had swung around, looking for the source of the commotion.

Her breath coming in short gasps, Iliana withdrew behind the tree, her gaze darting around the branches and trunks that surrounded her. There it was. It was that cursed black bird again. A raven, she thought. She had no doubt it was the same one. It perched on a half-denuded branch, watching her, its head cocked to one side.

She narrowed her eyes and hissed at it, then slowly looked around the tree again. Another figure was approaching over an intervening rise, fumbling with the front of his clothing. Iliana let out a long, low breath. The bird could not know what a favor it had just done her. There were four of them after all. If she had emerged from the trees when she had tried to, the fourth would have caught her unawares, probably warned the others. He too had a sword strapped at his hip. She watched as he approached the three men. He too was tall, brown hair to his shoulders, and across his shoulders, he carried a bundle. Iliana bit her lip. It was something wrapped in faded red cloth. She glanced back at the bird, but it had already departed.

"Aren't you lot ready yet?" he said in a rough voice. "Come on. Get moving." There was a confident swagger to his step as he neared.

Iliana thought quickly. As much as she relished the thought of giving these men their proper due, there was no way she could take them here in the open. She would have to find some other way to deal with them. Perhaps to take them one by one, but to do so without arousing the others' suspicions would be hard. She watched as they made ready their possessions and headed off over the hill, all the while grumbling abuse at each other. Thankfully, the direction they took kept them reasonably close to the tree line, so she was able to track them for a few hours without breaking cover.

Finally, toward early afternoon, they broke their trek, dumped their packs and pulled out provisions.

Good! She watched and waited. Even though she wasn't really paying attention to what they talked about, the few snatches that she did catch fueled her low opinion of them even more. A small finger of forest stretched out in front of them. She judged the distance and thought they were close enough to it to serve her purposes. One of the men, the one Rat-Face had called Haron, belched and clambered to his feet. He looked around, muttered something to his companions, then lumbered toward the trees, close to the spot where Iliana stood in concealment. If this was to work, she had to act quickly.

She was holding her breath, intent on the man's next actions, when a noise from above grabbed at her attention. She glanced up quickly. The cursed bird was back again. She bared her teeth at it. She couldn't have it interfere now. What was it doing following her anyway? She turned her focus back to the approaching ruffian, praying silently that the bird would keep its place.

As he entered the trees, already working at the ties on his stained leather trousers, she shrank back out of sight. Gently, she eased her knife from her belt. She couldn't afford for this one to make any noise. He only walked a few paces before he started to squat, but before he was half way through the action, Iliana was upon him. He grunted as he felt her hand curl around his shoulder, but that was the last real sound he made. She drew her knife quickly across his throat, pressing one knee against his back for extra purchase.

The man fell like a sack, clutching at his throat, his eyes wide. Iliana felt no compunction. She had done similar putting a wounded beast out of its misery. The warm smell of blood was around her, and she shook her head and stepped back. There was no regret in what she'd just done, but there was no satisfaction, either. She frowned as she watched him die, wondering at the lack of feeling, then stepped quickly back to see what the other three were doing. They were still squatting in a semicircle, waiting, she thought. Rat-Face had his legs stretched out in front of him, leaning back on his hands.

Quick action was even more important now. Iliana made her rapidly to the stand of trees jutting to one side of their group. Noting each of their positions, she drew her sword and took a deep breath, steeling herself. There would be no warning. She charged.

Iliana ran at full speed, her sword held aloft. The men were just starting to turn as she reached their position. She brought her blade down, slashing to one side, catching Rat-Face in the thigh as she passed. He toppled to the side, clutching at his wounded leg, squawling like a baby. The other two were scrabbling for their weapons as she spun, ready to slash again. Slowly, the two remaining men got to their feet. Rat-Face lay on the ground where she had hit him, blubbering.

The one with the scar glanced at his other companion, the man with the rough voice. He was waving his sword back and forth, a cruel grin on his face.

"Well, what have we here?" he said. There was nothing about his tone that Iliana liked.

Iliana, her body feeling charged, her breath coming quickly, saw that leering face and felt the anger wash through her anew. She took a deliberate step forward. He gestured to the one with the scar to move around to her side. She glanced at him and narrowed her eyes. The whimpering sound from the man on the ground broke through to her. She couldn't afford to let her fury rule her.

"I want no more hurt here," she said through clenched teeth. "You have taken something that is not yours. I have come to take it back."

"Have you now? So, the old witch has sent you, has she?"

Before the last word was out of his lips, he lunged, but Iliana was ready for him. She sidestepped the thrust, and whirled, bringing her sword up to block a slashing blow from her side. The impact went right through her blade and shook her arm, but she turned rapidly, blocking another thrust from the first man.

"Give it back and it's finished," she said.

"It'll be finished long before then," said the first, grinning evilly with bared teeth.

There was a flicker in his eyes, and Iliana spun to the left, barely bringing up her blade in time to block a wicked down stroke from the man with the scar. Iliana knew what to do. She fell to one knee, as if the stroke had driven her to the ground. The scarred ruffian was leaning forward into his stroke. In one quick move, Iliana thrust up with her other hand, burying her small knife in his belly. He fell back, clutching at the hilt, a look of shock on his face. In an instant she was on her feet, her sword at the ready.

The first one was regarding her warily now. "You will pay for this," he said with a growl, and charged. There was no smile there now. She could see the rage on his face. She danced out of the way of his charge. Flustered he turned, his face contorting. He charged again. Iliana stepped lightly back, drawing him in. He lifted his sword high, ready to bring it down in a skull-crushing blow, but as he did so, he left himself exposed. Iliana thrust forward, catching him in the chest. Her sword slid deep. With a heave, she pulled it free.

The man, at the top of his upswing, staggered back, dropped his sword behind him and collapsed to his knees. With a strangled growl, he fell to the side.

Iliana looked around at her handiwork. Rat-Face was still whimpering, huddled where she had left him. The one with the scar was groaning weakly, hands clutched to his belly, blood leaking out between his fingers. It wasn't enough. She would finish the job. She glanced over at the red-wrapped bundle. There was her prize, but she hadn't finished yet. She saw the Old Mother lying there on the ground, the marks of violence on her face, and her rage welled up in her anew. She strode over the where Rat-Face lay, looking up at her, fear painted over his wide-eyed face. She lifted her sword.

"P-please," he said. "Please."

She hesitated, seeking sense from the conflicting urges warring inside her. A croaking cry came from somewhere far up in a tree, and she glanced over. She looked down at the man, whimpering on the ground below her.

"P-please. I have children. I have a family."

Slowly, Iliana lowered her sword.

She pointed at the man with the scar with her sword. "Go," she said to Rat-Face. "Take him with you. Find some better way to look after your family."

Rat-Face got unsteadily to his feet. Still looking fearfully at Iliana, he hobbled over to where the other man lay and helped him struggle to his feet, still clutching at his belly.

"Th-thank you," he said as he passed.

She watched them as they staggered and limped off out of the clearing, supporting each other. She did not know if the one with the scar would survive the gut wound, but if they got to a healer soon enough, he might. The knife was small, and it would not have gone deep. She had at least given him the chance of living. She stepped over and retrieved the knife, wiped it clean, and replaced it in her belt.

Suddenly feeling drained, she squatted on the ground and proceeded to wipe her sword clean on the grass beside her.

A raucous call from above grew her gaze skyward. The cursed black bird, again! It circled the clearing then swept down toward her. She gripped her sword hilt more tightly. If the bird was going to attack her again…

The bird alighted on the cloth-wrapped bundle and Iliana tried to shoo it away with a wave of her arm. The beast fluttered briefly upward, and then came to rest again, standing on the bundle. It fixed her with one shining eye. Iliana stood back up, her fists planted on her hips.

"What is it you want, bird?"

Her large, feathered tormenter hopped up and down the length of the bundle, and then cocked its head again. She lifted her sword. If the creature would not move, then she would move it.

The bird opened its beak. "Iliana," it croaked.

She shook her head. It had sounded like her name, but how could that be?

"Iliana," it said again.

She crouched then, a frown upon her brow. "Did you speak, bird?"

"Put down your sword."

With a gasp, she regained her feet and backed away a few steps, her blade held in the guard position. "Wh-what?" she said.

The bird stepped along the length of the bundle, spread its wings as if to take to the air again, then settled once more, its feather ruffled.

"The cursed things sometimes have a mind of their own," croaked the bird. "Put down your weapon, Iliana."

She glanced around, looking for some sort of trick, looking for who it was making sport of her, scanning the edges of the small clearing, searching for who stood hidden in the shadows of the trees.

"Will you listen, child?"

It was the bird, no question, and the voice was familiar. Her mouth gone dry, her heart pounding in her chest, she lowered her weapon and hesitantly placed it on the grass. She had to be sure. This could be some sort of trick.

"Who are you? What do you want?"

"You know who I am, child. What you did was well done, and I am pleased you have retrieved what I sent you for."

"Old Mother?" said Iliana.

"Yes, of course," said the bird. "Now listen to me. I cannot hold this creature for too much longer — willful thing."

The bird hopped off the bundle and stood looking at her, its head slightly cocked. "Take the package and open it. It would have been yours before long, but it is yours now. You have shown you are ready."

As Iliana stepped forward and reached down to the bundle, the bird hopped out of her way, its wings spreading as if preparing for flight again.

"Hurry, child," it said.

Iliana tore at the leather thongs wrapping the package, laid it on the ground and started slowly folding back the faded red cloth. There was some design on the material, but it was so faint she could barely make it out. Turning back the last flap of cloth, she gasped. There, revealed, lay a sword like no other she had seen. The hilt was finely worked, a serpent tightly coiled around the grip. The blade itself was silver, shining, a light green sheen evident in the metal. A scent washed up from the cloth, strange, like the smell of air before a storm.

"Pick it up, child."

"N-no. I couldn't," she said.

"Do as I tell you, Iliana. The sword is yours by right."

She reached forward gingerly, touching her fingers to the hilt. There was a slight tingle as her fingertips met the cold metal. And it was cold. Colder than it should have been, by rights. Surprised, she snatched her hand away.

"Go on," croaked the bird. "Pick it up."

Again, she reached for the blade, this time grasping it firmly. She lifted the sword, feeling the tingle in her arm, feeling the cold metal solid in her grasp. She stood, holding the sword before her. The weight was right, so right. She could feel the balance in the blade. The hilt molded to her grip, is if it were made for her. She held the weapon up, marveling at the strange green sheen, turning it in the light.

"Iliana," said the bird.

She tore her attention from the blade and turned to look at the creature standing there.

"I cannot hold this beast much longer. You have fought well, yet you mastered your anger. You showed mercy when it was necessary. It's as it should be. You have earned the blade. You will need that strength in times to come, because you have been chosen by the fates for this task, many summers past. I was shown that you were born to bear this blade, but you must do so with mercy and wisdom. Your anger could have ruled you, but you ruled it when it was needed. Know this weapon – it is Serpent's Kiss. Those who took it would have carried it to a man who would wield it in your stead. You have stopped that happening, for now."

The black bird squawked and hopped a few paces, its wings again making as if to beat the air.

"Be still, bird," it croaked. "I cannot stay too much more," it said. "Now, come back. Come back to me. We have much to talk about before you are finally ready to leave and follow your destiny."

With a mighty croak, the bird shot into the air, its wings beating, a single feather floating down to rest on the ground where it had stood. Iliana tracked it as it rose rapidly into the sky and disappeared from sight.

She looked down at the single feather, then back to the blade held before her, wondering at what had just happened.

"Serpent's Kiss," she said quietly, turning the blade this way and that, looking at the way the colors slid along its length.

Slowly, carefully, she placed it down on the faded cloth and wrapped the precious weapon. She tied what remained of the leather thongs around the bundle, holding the cloth secure, then stood and retrieving her own, old sword, slid it back in place behind her back. She still could not believe that such a weapon could be hers. She hefted the bundle beneath one arm. The Old Mother had said she was not ready, and inside, Iliana knew that the old woman was right. What did the Old Mother have planned for her? That was, if it was truly the Old Mother, and not some trickster in the shape of a bird. But she had the sword. That was proof enough.

As she turned and headed for the forest's edge, she knew that the Old Mother was right – they indeed had much to talk about.

-The End-

Responsibility

The pair of them lived, or rather they existed, in the old department store down on Catatonia Avenue, Death's Head and the Sickly Child. The glass fronts faced out onto bits and pieces and inside there was the same. The street had had another name once — a proper name. And the Sickly Child had The Virus, but Death's Head didn't mind. She'd seen The Virus plenty of times before and she knew it couldn't touch her.

Death's Head glanced across to where The Sickly Child was rooting around among the shoetrees and the mirrors, pushing aside cobwebs and dust with her pale thin hands. Her fine white hair made a cloud around her puffy milk-hued face. She hummed a tune as she moved from stack to stack, seeking something; Death's Head knew not what.

"What are you looking for?"

The Sickly Child's humming broke off. "Red shoes," she said. "I feel like some red shoes." She performed a little pirouette, her arms curved above her head. Dust motes sparkled in the shafts of liquid light as her faded floral dress billowed around her.

Death's Head pursed her lips. Her young companion would be looking for hours, and when she finally found her precious shoes, if she did, they'd occupy her for long enough. The Sickly Child was easily amused.

She turned away and left her to it. She picked her way over fallen shelves and tumbled displays toward the vast marble staircase leading to the lower floors. Small pieces of rubble crunched beneath her feet. She didn't care about the noise or who it might disturb — this was their place.

On the ground floor, the doors to the street hung open. One angled where it had been torn from its upper hinges, the thick glass long gone. Death's Head slipped between them and stood looking up and down the street. That way lay the ocean. She used to think about taking that long walk down to the seaside, and then she would just keep going. She would walk and walk, watching her life dissipate in a trail of whisper bubbles in the cool water above, waves sweeping back above her head. That had been before. Now she had The Sickly Child to look after. Now she had responsibilities.

In the other direction lay the mountains, looming large with their forbidding crags. They sat in the back of her awareness, a constant reminder of their isolation. Few had ventured that way. None had ever returned.

Some said the war had been a bad thing, but Death's Head didn't believe that. Once upon a time she'd been a nursing assistant, way back before the conflict, but now she was a doctor — a proper doctor. She gave her little black leather kit an appreciative shake. It had taken her months to build up her small supply of instruments and medications, scrounged from here and there. She fingered the small badge — her namesake — she wore to mark her position. The skull shape with its flying silver wings was pinned to her jacket, had been for years. It was hard to remember now, but she thought she'd found it in a bike shop a couple of blocks over.

The air was good this morning.

A figure lurched down the street toward her, and

she pressed back into the overhang. She watched him warily. His black wool cap was pulled down to his eyebrows. His stained brown coat flapped around him, and the bundled green sweater was bunched around his belly and chest. Ratty threads hung from its bottom. Under one arm he carried a large package, wrapped in black plastic and taped with wide strips. He carried that package everywhere. Death's Head sank back further against the wall as he drew close to her and passed, muttering to himself, without even a glance. The Dog Man was basically harmless, she knew, but he unsettled her. Nobody had ever bothered to ask, but the package he carried so religiously under his arm had the shape of a mid-sized dog. Though, why he'd want to walk around with a dog wrapped in black plastic, she had no idea.

Perhaps it had been a pet, something dear. Something from before.

Death's Head waited a few minutes until she was sure the Dog Man had gone, then stepped back out from the protective building shadow. Across the street lay another large, abandoned store, just like their own. That one had scaffolding still in place, ragged strips of plastic hanging from the metal structure like torn shrouds stirring lazily in the breeze. She often wondered what the building would have looked like without its ripped exterior. It was so hard to remember the times before, sometimes, that she just had to try and imagine. Her gaze lingered on the building, then shaking the thoughts away, she turned and headed up the street to perform her rounds.

No one knew where the first strike had come from. Some had said the Middle East, when there was a

Middle East. Chemical, biological, nobody had been sure. But none of that really mattered anymore. It was all the distant past. All that mattered was the life they had cobbled together on Catatonia Avenue.

Two blocks further on, she came upon a bus stop. A baby sat at the base of the sign, watching her with its wobbling gaze. She smiled to herself. Didn't it know that the buses were late? It bored with watching her and turned its head to face the other direction. As she neared, the baby teetered its head back to look at her. She stooped in front of it and held out a hand.

"What are you doing out here, little man?" she said.

It stared at her with big blue eyes then shoved its fist in its mouth.

"Yes," she said, looking up and down the street, then up at the sky. "It's a lovely day for a trip to the beach." And she thought again of cool, calm water, flowing gently above her head.

A quick scan of the surrounding buildings revealed no sign of the child's mother. What had Doris been thinking of, leaving the child out here like that? Death's Head got to her feet. She stood contemplating the surrounding storefronts. Perhaps the video arcade....

A quick call inside the doorway among the black-boxed silence revealed nothing. She peered around the gloom between the lifeless monoliths, but nothing moved. There was a supermarket across the street. Perhaps it would yield better results. She quickly crossed the street, ignoring the child that still watched her, and poked her head through the door.

"You in here?" she called. There was a scurry of

movement from behind one of the shelves, followed by silence.

"Come on out," said Death's Head reassuringly. "It's only me." Wide frightened eyes and the top of a face surrounded by stringy gray-blond hair cut in a bob appeared tentatively above the shelf.

"I thought it was *them*," said the woman.

Death's Head frowned. What was Doris talking about? "There's no one here but us crazies," she said and laughed.

Doris Day emerged, sliding slowly around the end of an aisle.

"What were you thinking of, Doris?" she asked. "Leaving Blue out there on the bus stop like that."

"I-I left him there for collection," said the woman. She stood, her eyes downcast. She wrung her hands in front of her. "M-maybe they'll take Blue and put him somewhere nice. Somewhere nicer than this. It's no good for me, but maybe Blue..."

Death's Head glanced back across the street, but Blue was sitting where she'd left him.

"Now, who exactly is going to collect Blue?" asked Death's Head, turning back to face her.

"Those people who came and took Puffing Billy away," she said.

"No one took Puffing Billy. I saw him up at the Plaza yesterday. Now you go and fetch Blue and take him inside. It's not good for him to be sitting out on the street like that."

"But they did. I saw them. They took Puffing Billy."

Doris appeared convinced of what she was saying.

It was unlike Doris to be convinced of anything.

"Describe them for me, Doris."

"I don't know." She shrugged. "Just people."

"Well, if they were just people, what would they want with Puffing Billy? And what would they want with Blue? Blue's your baby, Doris. You have to take better care of him."

Briefly, for the first time, Death's Head wondered who the father was. There were so few of them. It couldn't be the Dog Man. Surely not.

"Doris, I want you to go fetch Blue and go home. Will you do that for me?"

Doris bit her lip and nodded slowly, then sidled past and out onto the street. Death's Head turned and watched the gaunt figure while she retrieved her child, and clutching him to her narrow chest, disappeared inside one of the buildings opposite. Death's Head waited for a few moments to make sure she didn't reappear.

She could soon check if what Doris had said was true. Puffing Billy never left the Plaza. He chuffed around the hallways and into the grand rooms. The Plaza was only four blocks away. With a quick look to check that Doris hadn't thought to leave Blue out on the street again, she headed up the avenue.

Another block further up, a shape peered out from a doorway. Long white beard and cane. Old Ebenezer. She smiled at him and waved. He nodded furiously and waved his cane in greeting, then disappeared inside. She'd visit him later, on the way back. Normally she did them each in turn, maintaining a clear routine with her rounds, the proper way, but what Doris had told her made her uneasy. Old Ebenezer would wait.

It didn't take her long to get to the Plaza. She stood outside the tarnished revolving doors, listening, expecting to hear Billy's whistle echoing from inside the lobby, but the Plaza was silent. She pushed past the revolving doors, still miraculously with their glass intact, and walked to the lobby's center. Still nothing. Tall dead plants stood in square bronze pots, as tarnished as the doors, and bits of leaf and dirt lay scattered across the marble floor. Scuffmarks tracked across the tiles where Billy had pulled his imaginary carriages along his never-ending track.

"Billy?" she called.

Nothing.

He could be asleep, but Billy rarely slept.

She'd just have to check every floor. She headed for the staircase, and the upper floors, careful of her footing on the faded and holed carpet. She had been so used to the smooth marble staircase of the department store, that she'd tripped once, her toe catching in a rip as she pounded up the stairs. The bruise had been painful for a month.

Death's Head reached the next floor and listened again. There was no sign of the shuffle, shuffle, woooh-woooh of Billy's passage. Nor on the next floor, nor the next.

By the time she reached the hotel's top floor, she had given up hope of finding him. She listened carefully at each floor on the way back down, but the results were the same. There had to be a reason for Puffing Billy's absence. Nothing would drag him away from his beloved hotel. Death's Head had to think.

She crossed to one of the cracked leather chairs strewn about the lobby and sat. The creaking chair echoed loudly in the silence.

No Puffing Billy. Doris leaving Blue out for collection. She'd seen Old Ebenezer. But where were the others? The Dog Man was okay. She'd seen him too. But if what Doris said was true, then someone had taken Puffing Billy away. No one she knew could do that, *would* do that. They were *all* her responsibility. Most of them could look after themselves with a little helpful prompting, except for the Sickly Child. But the Sickly Child had Death's Head to look after her. Even though Puffing Billy thought he was a train, at least he could look after himself. He'd know better than to let someone take him away, wouldn't he?

The Sickly Child was a different matter.

It just didn't make sense.

Then it struck her. The Sickly Child!

Death's Head had left the Sickly Child alone in the department store. If there was someone wandering around removing people with no explanation....

It was *her* responsibility.

She leaped up from the chair, and fumbling her kit, raced out the door.

Seven blocks. Seven whole blocks.

By the time she reached the department store where they lived, her breath was coming in ragged gasps and the blood was pounding in her ears. She dragged herself to a stop, barely able to believe what she saw. Parked in front of the store, sat a big white van. It looked like no other vehicle she had ever seen on Catatonia Avenue. The paintwork was clean and the bodywork undamaged.

Nervously she crept around the van's back corner, keeping low. Plucking up her courage, she popped her head up and glanced through the van windows. It was empty. She swallowed back her nerves and stood, looking for movement on the surrounding street. Still nothing. They had to be inside the store. And inside was the Sickly Child — alone.

Death's Head stifled a curse and charged toward the hanging doors of her home.

They were standing there when she reached the second floor, a man and a woman. Something was strange about the way they were dressed. They wore black uniforms, but that wasn't it. Then she realized. The clothes were all crisp and clean. They wore hats as well, each one with a thick red band and a shiny silver badge in the shape of a shield on front. Their faces were clean and shiny too, just like the badges. Between them, stood the Sickly Child. She smiled when she saw Death's Head.

"Look," she said, pointing down at her feet. Her face was glowing. She'd found her red shoes and wore them now, all bright and sparkling. They looked strangely out of place in all the gray and dust. The light from the windows behind made a nimbus of her thin white hair.

Death's Head took in the scene immediately. The man and the woman looked wrong here; they did not belong. This was *her* place.

"Who are you?" she said. "What do you want?"

"We're here to help," said the man. He held the Sickly Child gently by one arm. The woman held the other.

"From the Salvation Army," said the woman.

At the mention of armies, Death's Head took a step back. But that wasn't right. There was something about salvation. She bit her lip.

"We just want to help," continued the woman. "We've come to take you away from here, to somewhere better."

"Yes," said the Sickly Child. "We're going home." She clicked her heels together and grinned a stupid grin.

"No," said Death's Head. "We like it fine just here. Why now? Why after so long?"

"It took a while for things to get back in balance," said the man. "We're only now starting to pick up the pieces."

Death's Head took another step backward.

"There's nothing to be afraid of," said the woman, lifting a calming hand. "If you just come with us, everything will be all right. Proper medical treatment. A warm place to stay. Proper food."

Death's Head looked at the three of them standing there, the crisp black uniforms, the Sickly Child's idiot smile in her too-pale face. She couldn't. How could anything be all right? What did they mean, *proper* medical treatment?

"No!" she cried. Clutching her kit to her chest, she turned and ran. She ran past the tumbled shelves, between empty display cases, over broken glass and brick. She ran toward the broad marble staircase leading to the upper floors. Up and away — away to the roof.

"Wait!" said the voice, echoing behind her. She heard the Sickly Child giggle.

She burst out onto the rooftop, thrusting the metal door open with a crash. Birds scattered into the air, wings whirring and flapping about her, dust and feathers flying in a cloud.

Her heart pounding in her chest, she crept to the roof edge, listening for pursuit, but none came. Then she heard noises from the street below.

She watched them from the rooftop, peering over the edge as they led the Sickly Child out into their big white van. They didn't even look up. She watched as they drove away up Catatonia Avenue, weaving slowly between the few discarded vehicles that lay battered by the roadside and the bits and pieces strewn across the street. She lay there panting, staring down at where the van had turned, long after it had disappeared from view. The van had gone. The Sickly Child was gone.

She didn't move from her spot until darkness had shadowed the empty street.

For most of the night, she wandered, roaming the floors of the big empty department store, waiting for the Sickly Child to return. Only her own footsteps echoed from the hollow walls. At any moment, she expected the Sickly Child's humming or one of her meaningless songs to come drifting from some veiled corner. Finally, she slept, alone, curled up in the corner where the Sickly Child had been seeking her magic red shoes.

The next day she searched. She searched the vacant buildings and the empty streets. Twice she saw the big white van and ducked out of view, clutching her kit to her chest, until the van had passed. Once she saw the Dog Man, no one else. Though she looked, there was not a trace of anyone. They were all gone: Puffing Billy,

Doris Day, Blue, Old Ebenezer, and the others. And the Sickly Child. All of them.

By the third day, she had given up hope of finding them again, and the van had stopped coming. There was still the Dog Man, but that wasn't anywhere near what she wanted, what she needed. She simply couldn't stomach the thought of him being the only one. The Dog Man and his black plastic package. Nothing else. How could she survive with that?

She looked around, up and down the empty street, and slowly, slowly, the realization came. All she had left was the ocean.

Gently, carefully, she stooped and placed the bag containing her scavenged kit down at her feet, her mind made up. Then, just as slowly, she stood, turned toward the beach and saw....

Further down the avenue toward the beach, in the middle of the street, stood the Dog Man. The light made it difficult to see, but she knew it was the Dog Man because of his package. It stood on the road beside him, a dog-shaped silhouette. He was waving something at it and muttering. Then he threw what he was waving.

A stick shape arced out and up into the sky, sailing through the air to land further down the street. Where had he found a stick?

The Dog Man stood watching the place where the stick had fallen, turned, placed his hands on his hips and muttered something to his packaged companion. Then, with a shrug of his shoulders, he wandered off to retrieve the stick. He left his black plastic shape standing there, alone, in the middle of the street.

A few moments later, the Dog Man returned

carrying the stick with him. He stooped a little, waved the stick in front of the place where the package's head would be, then threw. Out and up, the stick sailed into the air and fell to the street. The Dog Man stood waiting. Nothing.

Three times Death's Head watched the performance. Three times the Dog Man threw his stick, waited, then went and brought it back. And by the third time, despite her doubts, Death's Head realized that she knew something else. Watching that display, the actions filled with a hopeless futility, she had come to an understanding.

With a slight smile, she reached down and carefully lifted her kit from the spot where she had placed it. She clutched it protectively against her chest, smiling still as the Dog Man threw once more. Her smile grew more certain as she headed down the street toward him. He wasn't quite the same, with his ratty clothes and stringy hair, but he could almost be the Sickly Child — almost.

-The End-

Wings of the Gods

Sprawled between two wooden pallets, half in a shining pool of scum-coated oily water lay a youth, naked as the day he was born. Jackson stopped in mid step and gazed down on the vision in front of him. Well muscled, perfectly proportioned, the youth was just lying there. He seemed to be breathing. His eyes were closed. From what Jackson could see, he didn't appear injured. Jackson crouched with difficulty and peered closer. How did a young man like this end up naked and abandoned in some dirty back alley with not a mark on him? He looked quickly from one end of the alley to the other. It was dark and it was late. There was no one to see. He could just ignore it and go on about his way, minding his own business. He was about to do just that, pushing himself upright with a grunt, when the boy moaned. Jackson swallowed, torn. What should he do? The youth's eyes fluttered open. They were bright in the darkness, and they fixed him with a look that seemed to pin him where he was. One hand rose, wavering before him, reaching out. Jackson swallowed again. He thought then what his morality would have him do, what he really should do if he had a shred of conscience and reluctantly, he knew the answer. He reached out for the hand and helped the youth to his feet.

"What are you doing here?" Jackson asked, peering into his face.

The youth appeared completely oblivious to his own nakedness and frowning, was scanning the ground, as if seeking something.

"What is it?" asked Jackson. "What are you looking for?"

"I've lost my shoes," he said. The voice was like music.

"It seems like you've lost more than your shoes," said Jackson. "Are you okay?"

Jackson received a frown in response, as if what he'd just said made no sense. The young man shook his head and continued searching the ground.

"Listen, you can't stay here like this." Jackson pulled off his coat and tried to drape it around the young man's shoulders. He seemed completely heedless of the cold, and simply tried to shrug it off.

"My shoes," he said again. "I need them."

Eventually Jackson managed to hang the coat awkwardly around the young man's shoulders, those perfect shoulders.

"We can't stay here," he said. "You'd better come with me. Is there someone we can call? Family? Friends? Someone?"

All he got in return was a blank look.

Jackson sighed and reached up with one hand to place gentle pressure on one shoulder and steer the young man towards the alley's end. From whence had come this milk of human kindness, he wondered. Jackson normally didn't do anything for anybody. At least not any more. Was it simply the fact that this…child…was so perfectly formed in such contrast to his own grotesque and aging frame? The tall lithe body, the tight blonde curls, the muscled calves, he watched them all as he guided the young man down the alley and out across the street, quickly scanning at the alley's end to ensure that they were not being observed.

Not without some protest or fuss, Jackson finally managed to shepherd him along the street, along the next block and up the narrow sets of stairs where he fumbled with his keys for a couple of seconds, not really knowing what he was going to do next.

As soon as he got inside the door, the youth shrugged off Jackson's coat and simply let it fall to the floor. He stood naked in the apartment's centre, looking around at the bare walls and the rude furnishings. Finally, he turned to fix Jackson with that bright blue gaze.

"Who are you?" he said.

Jackson cleared his throat. "Perhaps I should ask you the same thing. My name is Jackson. Jackson Fuchs."

There was no reaction, well not what Jackson had expected. Usually there was the suppressed snicker, the biting of the tongue, but this time, nothing. Merely a simple blink of acknowledgement.

"I'm sorry," said Jackson. "I don't think I have any clothes that will fit you. Wait here." He disappeared into the small space that served as his bedroom, pulled a blanket from the bed, and held it out as he re-entered the living room. "At least put this on."

The young man took the blanket, again with that frown and managed to drape it around his lithe frame.

"Well, you can tell me your name, can't you?" said Jackson.

"You can call me … um, Harry…" He paused and peered into Jackson's face. "Jackson Fuchs." He looked around himself again. "I need to piss."

"Through there," said Jackson, pointing.

He watched as the young man calling himself Harry found the bathroom door and stood unashamedly in front of the toilet and urinated noisily. Jackson had no illusions that it was not the young man's real name, but Harry would do for now.

The boy didn't bother flushing and Jackson frowned. He wandered back into the room uncaringly, the blanket already starting to slip off.

"Um, Harry. How did you get there? Did something happen? Are you sure you're all right?"

All the time, Jackson's gaze was roving over the sleek body before him. He couldn't help but moisten his lips. He shook his head, as much at his own action as to clear his focus, and not without a touch of trouble, met the boy's eyes.

Harry, who was still studying Jackson's small apartment, waved a hand dismissively. "It is a lengthy tale. Too long for now, I think," he said. Again, the melodious quality of his voice struck Jackson. There was some sort of accent, but he couldn't pick it, and the turn of phrase was a little odd as well. Something you might say…perhaps he was from the theatre. A gorgeous young actor. That would fit. For a moment, Jackson's hopes fluttered in his chest.

"Listen, you sit. Let me get you something hot to drink. A tea, a coffee? And then we can sort out what we're going to do with you. So, what will it be?"

The boy calling himself Harry frowned again.

"Tea or coffee?"

He shook his head.

"All right. Coffee it is. Do you want milk or sugar in it?"

"Honey. Do you have honey?"

Honey in coffee? Not the normal response. He thought he had some honey stashed in a cupboard somewhere.

"Yes, I think I have some. You sit right there. I will only be a couple of minutes."

On the way back into his kitchenette, Jackson detoured to attend to the toilet. Harry simply seemed not to notice.

Jackson fussed about, boiling water, ferreting about in the cupboards till he located the promised honey. He peered down at the jar. It was not too far gone, had not fully crystallised yet. He couldn't for the life of him remember the last time he'd had a use for honey. From time to time, he glanced back into the living room to check on his unexpected guest. Harry seemed to be muttering to himself. More than once, Jackson picked out the word 'shoes.'

He ferried two coffees back to the living room and handed the sweetened mug to Harry and then sat in the chair opposite, watching as the young man lifted the mug, sniffed at it, sipped tentatively, frowned, and then sipped again. Jackson wished he would do something about the way the blanket continued to slip further and further off exposing ever greater expanses of taut, tanned skin...

"What's wrong? Is it all right?" It wasn't the best coffee, but it was okay and something warm and sweet should be very welcome after waking up naked in a cold alley or so he would have thought.

Harry nodded and took another sip. He wasn't telling him a lot. Nonetheless, Jackson had come to a decision, despite his natural misgivings.

"Listen, Harry," said Jackson. "It's late. You're welcome to stay here tonight. I'll get you a pillow. You can sleep here, on the couch. I don't know where you have come from or what else I can do for you. We can sort all that out in the morning."

Harry looked at him blankly. Not a word of appreciation. Nothing.

It had been a long time since Jackson had had anyone at his apartment. Usually, he wouldn't bring people back here. Since his last true relationship, not much had happened and that was more than three years now. It was what happened when you got older. Oh sure, there were those brief and somewhat seamy encounters, all too few and far between, in places out of the public eye, though technically those places too were public, but he'd never been motivated to ask someone back to his place, the place where he lived. Not until now, that was, and this was a completely different circumstance altogether. Maybe he was being foolish? He looked around his modest space. There really wasn't anything here to take. Anyway, a naked thief should be pretty easy to spot, even in this neighbourhood.

Making sure that Harry was settled, Jackson retired to the bedroom. The night passed slowly and torturously…the boy was beautiful. Once or twice, awake and sleep flitting from his grasp, he considered getting up and making his way to the couch, crouching down beside it, reaching out…but he managed to resist. Finally, he pulled the covers up around his shoulders and buried his head in the pillow. It did nothing to chase away the thoughts. Eventually, he drifted into sleep.

He was awake with the morning light slicing through the edges of his blinds, and stumbled out of the bedroom rubbing his eyes, only to find Harry there where he had left him, wide awake and muttering to himself. A quick scan of the apartment saw that nothing had been shifted. It looked like Harry had not moved at all either.

"Did you sleep?" he asked.

Harry shook his head. "I don't sleep much."

It was the most cogent thing Jackson had had from him.

"I must find my shoes."

"Listen, I didn't see anything where I found you. Looking at you, I don't think there's anything of mine that will fit. If you like, I will get you something to wear, and then we'll go and look together." There was a sports store a couple of blocks over. He could pick up something loose, stretchable, and cheap. Some sweats maybe. As much of a pity as it was to cover up that body. "Just let me shower and I'll see what I can get. Meanwhile, you might see about making some coffee. Everything's there in the kitchen."

He showered, slipped into the bedroom, and threw on the clothes. By the time he was ready and moved back into the kitchen area, Harry was standing there, blanket draped casually over his shoulders staring blankly at the shelf. There was no sign of coffee.

"What's wrong?" asked Jackson.

"I didn't know what…." The voice trailed off.

Jackson sighed. He supposed he would have to make his own coffee. As he pushed past the young man, he tried to ignore the quick, cold rush of excitement in his abdomen as they made fleeting contact. Damn. He coughed and set about making coffee, keeping his back firmly turned to the boy. He didn't want to look at him. Not right now. By the time he'd finished with the coffee, and handed a sweetened version to Harry, he was able to look at him again as he sipped his own. It was too hot, but he finished it quickly, wanting to get to the shop so he could at least put some clothes on the boy before it became even more awkward than it was already.

It took him about an hour to walk to the store, browse through the goods and select something in dark blue that he thought would fit. The fabric had enough stretch in it that he guessed it would work even if he'd been wrong about the size. He took his time walking back to the apartment, considering his next steps. It would be best, he thought, if he got Harry dressed and got him outside. Looking for the missing shoes was as good an excuse as any.

When he stepped through the door, shopping bag in one hand, and keys still in the other, he was brought up short. What the…?

Harry was lying back on the couch, minus the blanket, stroking his erect penis in full view.

Jackson swallowed and coughed. "I'm sorry…I…"

"Do you not do this?" said Harry, with a slight frown. "I can show you how. I taught my son how to do this. It is pleasurable."

Jackson wasn't quite sure what he was most surprised about. He chose the latter. "You have a son?" He barely seemed old enough.

"Yes," said Harry, ceasing the ministrations and sitting back upright. The evidence of his activities still stood up, pointing almost in Jackson's direction. "Ugly little brute, with those hairy legs and those two nubbins on his head." He pointed to his forehead. "And what did he do? Went right out and taught the shepherds how to do it too. I showed him for him, not a group of dirty shepherds."

"Wait," said Jackson. "Shepherds? Nubbins?" He felt more comfortable walking right inside the living room now; the object of his focus was beginning to subside. He tossed the shopping bag across, and Harry deftly plucked it from the air and opened it to look inside.

"Put those on…please," said Jackson.

Harry slipped on the sweats as Jackson watched. A real pity in a way, but by now it was absolutely necessary. The talk of a son had cooled his speculation just a little. The sooner he got the boy out of the apartment and doing something else, the better things were going to be.

"I'm sorry. I don't have any shoes that will fit you."

"Shoes!" Harry looked even more like a golden youth decked out in the blue sweats. They fit loosely, but beneath them, his shape was unmistakable, including, Jackson thought, a particular shape. He swallowed.

"Yes," he said. "Let's go and find your shoes."

Harry was already halfway to the door.

The alley was as dingy and stinking as Jackson remembered it. He couldn't even recall what had possessed him to wander through it late at night. Harry was already sniffing around, pulling things aside, peering behind stacks of things and under crates and boxes. Jackson merely stood and watched, wincing a little with each splash and squelch made by Harry's bare feet in the muck.

To be honest, he was still a little distracted still by the whole masturbation thing.

After a time, Harry stood and looked at the sky with a sigh. He stayed that way for almost a minute.

"Well?" said Jackson.

"They are not here," Harry replied, lowering his gaze.

"Come on," said Jackson, with a sigh of his own. "We will take you shopping. I haven't got very much, but we should get you some shoes. You haven't even told me what they look like. Are they shoes, boots? I guess anything will do now."

"No," said Harry. "Not anything will do. My shoes are different. They are like gilded sandals."

Gilded…

"Um. I think we need to go to a different part of town."

Gilded sandals. More and more Harry was turning into a mass of contradictions and again, Jackson was uncertain. As he led Harry down the street and towards the main shopping strip—a place he didn't go very much with its designer stores and upmarket boutiques—he was chewing it over. Along the way, he glanced once or twice at Harry's face, studying the firm jaw, the clear blue gaze, the well-formed nose. He looked like he had purpose.

They were halfway down the first block when Harry stopped in his tracks and turned, slowly and then burst into laughter. Jackson followed his gaze but could not see for the life of him what would be so amusing. They were standing before a designer store, a bright red patterned silk scarf draped across each window display. There were mannequins decked in labelled goods and shoes, accessories, other things. He frowned and shook his head.

"What is it?"

Harry laughed again and pointed up at the sign above the doorway.

Hermes.

Jackson frowned.

"But wait," said Harry leaning forward to peer a little more closely at the display. "There."

Jackson walked over and looked in at the window. A pair of gold sandals sat at the front of the display. They were women's sandals, obviously, but that didn't seem to matter to Harry. He was up against the glass, his hands on either side of his face staring down at them.

"Perhaps they will do," he said.

Jackson looked at the price tag and swallowed. "Perhaps we can find something like those further down," he said.

"No!" said Harry, swinging around to face him. "It must be those. Those I can do something with."

Jackson bit his lip. Against his better instincts, he allowed himself to be led into the store. He looked around nervously as the sales assistant eyed them, trying to decide whether they were worth approaching or even acknowledging.

"Um, excuse me," he said. "Those gold sandals in the window. My friend would like to see them."

The sales assistant approached sceptically looking them up and down, pausing on Harry's bare feet. She seemed to come to her senses a moment later. Perhaps, thought Jackson, she had decided that they were eccentric millionaires or something. She studied the feet for a moment.

"You have quite small feet for a man," she said. "Perhaps we have a size that fits. If you would like to wait here?"

Jackson watched her retreating back, wondering to himself whether she was going to find a shoebox out the back or call someone. Harry was standing where he was, scanning all the corners of the store.

"Why do they call themselves that?" he said. "Hermes..."

"I don't know," said Jackson. "It's a brand; that's all. Maybe there's some history to it."

Harry smiled. "Oh, I am sure there is history. It is a good name."

He had a great smile. A gorgeous smile. Jackson looked away.

The assistant returned after a short time. "Here, please sit and try these. They are the largest we have."

Harry did as he was instructed, slipped on the sandals not without a bit of difficulty and then stood and flexed his legs.

"Yes," he said.

"Um…."

"Yes," he said more forcefully turning to look at Jackson directly, fixing him with that clear blue gaze.

Jackson sighed. He'd seen the price. What the hell was he doing? He had to be out of his mind.

"Okay, we'll take them," he said. "Don't bother wrapping them."

He dug out his rarely used credit card, wincing as she swiped it and rang up the sale.

"Would you like the box? At least take the special bag for protection."

"Okay, just the bag," he said.

She handed it over and Jackson took Harry's arm and led him outside. The assistant was still watching them through the window and just in case he quickened his pace down the street. As they walked, Harry reached for the protective bag and looked at it.

"Hermes," he said and laughed. "Can I take this?"

"Take it? Take it where?"

Harry stopped. He turned and looked at Jackson and held the look. "I have to leave now. I can leave now."

There was a brief sense of relief for Jackson, and yet there was disappointment.

"But where will you go? I didn't think you had anywhere to go."

Harry glanced up at the sky. "Oh, I have many places to go." He looked up and down the street and then seemed to spot something. He grasped Jackson's arm and led him down to a small cut away alcove, deep enough to shield them from direct view of the rest of the street. He drew him inside.

Jackson's heart was beating strongly now. What was the boy doing?

Harry reached down and slipped the sandals off again. He held them up, and in turn inspected them closely. He placed them on the ground in front of him. Then, unhurriedly, he started to peel off the sweats.

"What are you doing?" Jackson said to him in a forced whisper. He glanced at the alcove's opening. Someone could come by at any moment. As much as he thought....

"Shhhh," said Harry, standing now, completely naked before him.

He reached down for the sandals and slipped them on, then passed his hands carefully over each one in turn.

Jackson wasn't quite sure what he was seeing. They were the same sandals, and yet.... something strange had happened at the back of them, as if they had sprouted...wings? He closed his eyes and opened them again. No, he wasn't imagining it.

Harry then reached down for the bag, held it up and laughed again. "Hermes," he said again to himself and then balled the fabric in his hand.

"I must leave now," he said, looking at Jackson straight in the face. "If you get bored or lonely after I have gone, remember what I showed you."

Jackson nearly choked. When he had recovered a little, he looked at Harry up and down, looked at the sandals, how they had changed and knew what he had started to know some time ago, but couldn't admit to himself.

"But..." he said to Harry. Was he dreaming?

"Don't worry," he told Jackson. "We will be together again soon. I will not forget what you've done. And I must admit to having a little fun with you." He smiled. "But then, that is what I do."

Jackson was confused. "What do you mean? How will we be together?" Could he really hope beyond hope?

Harry moved his face closer, grasped Jackson's chin gently with one hand and looked deeply into his eyes, searching first one pupil and then the other. "It will not be too long. I think about eighteen months as you measure time. I will be here for you and for you alone, Jackson. I will be there to help you on your journey. It will help repay your kindness."

"My jour—oh…," he said.

And with that, Harry was gone. A vague shimmering stirred in the air where he had stood. Feeling almost pathetic doing so, Jackson grasped feebly at sparkling motes as they faded back to the small alcove's dimness. Where moments before had been the taste of honey in the air, there was the musty smell of old water and garbage. He turned away, stepped out of the alcove, paused for a few seconds, and then sighing, walked back down the length of the street, slightly used and empty sweats in his hands. It wouldn't take him long to walk home, and when he did, he could remember. He held the sweats to his face and breathed in their odour. Even there was the hint of honey. He would remember that beautiful boy, he was sure of that, but he'd also be anticipating.

As he slowly walked the final block back to his apartment, he was clutching the empty garments to his chest, thinking not only about magic, but also about loss. Eighteen months was not very long.

-The End-

Stone Feather

Rain. Perpetual—drizzling down the panes of the environment hut. The leaden sky dragged at the consciousness and sapped energy, leaving him listless and depressed. Blake d'Alban turned the sample over and over in his fingers trying to make sense of it. Long, narrow, and veined, it could have been an arrowhead or maybe a fossilized feather. Clearly, it wasn't going to speak to him. He looked up and out of the window, seeing through the tiny rivulets to the lush green canopy beyond.

A chapaqua monkey leapt between the trees and disappeared from view. Three months now, and the chapaquas were the most advanced indigenous life form they had found. The curious little blue-gray creatures stole from the camp occasionally, when d'Alban or the others of the survey team forgot to lock things away, but apart from that, they were harmless. They moved in social groups, but they'd shown no evidence of tool use. That was about all they knew of them. Blake sighed. They certainly weren't capable of crafting anything as advanced as the sample he now held. He placed it carefully on the bench in front of him, pulled out a cigarette and lit it.

Estrella came up behind him. "You had any luck with that thing yet?" she asked, fanning the trail of his smoke away with one hand and giving him a disapproving look.

"No, nothing." He held the cigarette off to the side,

so the smoke wasn't rising in her face. "All I know for sure is that it isn't natural. Someone or something made it." He picked up the sample again and held it out. "You see those striations there? I reckon they're evidence of tooling—like someone's used a really fine machine to shape it. I won't know for sure until we can get it to the labs back home for dating and some more analysis."

"Uh-huh. Well, good luck, Blake. Maybe the survey party's had more success with the caves."

Blake replaced the sample, took another drag on his cigarette, and took a moment to admire Estrella's finely sculpted cheekbones and the deep olive skin running down under the neck of her coveralls. She ran her fingers through short-cropped red hair and stared out the window at the rain.

"When are they due back?" he asked.

"Oh, another couple of hours. Last they called in, there was nothing to report yet. Christ, when's this godammed rain going to stop?"

"Rhetorical question, right?"

"Yeah."

Estrella gave a thin smile. "I can always hope." She shoved her hands into her pockets and stood, rocking gently back and forth to the drumming rain rhythm on the shelter roof.

Blake turned back to the sample and picked it up. He turned it under the desk lamp for the hundredth time. Maybe, just maybe, he'd missed something.

"You know 'Strell? I don't even know what this thing's made of. It might be stone. It's not metal. I don't know. It's like some sort of really hard plastic or something. I have no idea how it came to be in the caves."

"Well, we're not going to find out here. Put it away and wait until you get home. It'll be your great find." She turned away from the window and stood looking down at him. "Anyway, I've got things to do. Let me know if you go out, okay? And don't forget to take your locator with you this time."

She rested her hand briefly on his shoulder, then turned and walked into the connecting tube that ran between the huts. Blake turned to watch the way her coveralls hugged her backside as she walked from the hut, then turned back to the desk with a sigh. Well and truly beyond his reach, but it was nice to dream. She was right, though. He wasn't going to find any answers by sitting and staring at the thing. He put it down again and rubbed the back of his neck. Maybe he should go up to the caves and give the others a hand.

Blake ground his cigarette out and tossed its remains outside the door of the hut. Estrella would shoot him if she caught him doing it, but what the hell. One little cigarette end wasn't going to wipe out an entire ecosystem. And in the months after they'd left to return to Earth with their reports, there'd be plenty of time for it to break down. He grabbed his rain-slicker from behind the door and thumbed the communicator switch.

"Listen 'Strell, I'm going up to the caves and see if the others need a hand. Okay?"

"Yeah, sure. Don't forget your—"

"—locator. Yep, I know, Mama Estrella. I've got it right here." He pocketed it and pulled the slicker on over his head. He was just about to step out when he saw a movement outside the door. One of the chapaquas had dashed across the clearing, grabbed his cigarette butt, and raced back to the shelter of the forest wall. If he hadn't seen it for himself, he wouldn't have believed it.

"Cheeky bugger," he muttered. He tried to see where it had gone, but there was no trace. Clearly, he'd have to be more careful. He shook his head and stepped out into the mud, rain thundering in his ears.

The canopy gave some shelter, but large, solid drops smacked down from the treetops onto his head. He tried to plot a path to avoid the bigger streams cascading down from above. His boots would be soaked by the time he got up to the caves, but at least he'd be out of the constant drumming. If he stood out here too long, he'd go deaf. Back home, he used to really like the big rainstorms, but when this stint was over, and the team returned home, he'd never walk in the rain again.

Just as he rounded a corner, a chapaqua stepped out on the path in front of him. Blake thought he recognized it from its markings. If so, it was a frequent visitor to the campsite. Blake stood still, waiting to see what it would do. The chapaqua watched him with large yellow eyes.

Standoff.

The raindrops fell on both of them, slapping the leaves and the thick oiled material of his slicker. The chapaqua didn't seem bothered by the rain. The water struck its short bluish fur and shattered into a myriad of smaller droplets. It folded long arms across its chest and tilted its head to one side.

Finally, the chapaqua became bored, scratched behind its head, and took off into the undergrowth. Blake stood and watched the spot where it had disappeared, thinking. The chapaqua almost seemed as if it had been watching him, seeing what he was going to do. No, it couldn't have been. Blake shook his head and slogged forward to the caves.

The steep climb to the cave mouth was treacherous with slippery leaves and moss-covered stones. Blake watched his footing carefully on the way up. There was a lip that ran round the hood edge of his slicker, ensuring that no water dripped into his eyes, but the constant rain drumming against the back of his head beat against his patience. He could hardly wait to get to the shelter of the caves.

The path wound on and up. The vegetation thinned as he neared the top, but the path was still slippery beneath his boots. He was watching his footing so carefully, that when he looked up and saw the chapaqua standing at the top looking down at him, he almost slipped in his surprise. Blake stopped still and frowned. Something was going on. Two chapaquas in the space of a few minutes. Normally they took off at the first sign of any of the survey team.

"What's going on, little fellow?" he said. "What's special about today?"

The chapaqua looked at him and tilted its head to the side, then back the other way. They were very like monkeys or maybe little furry people. Blake grinned at the image it conjured.

"Well, either you've got to move, or we're going to stand here all day. What's it going to be?" Briefly he wondered whether it was the same one from down below. The markings were similar. He thought perhaps it was.

He could see the cave mouth, the lip of the path, and the chapaqua standing above him. There were no trees to give protection at this end of the path and the rain beating against his head was really starting to annoy him. All he wanted was to get inside. If the chapaqua didn't move, he was going to have to do something about it.

He stood for a few moments longer, then muttered at it through gritted teeth. "Come on, move, will you?"

Blake lifted his arms and waved at it, trying to shoo it away, but it stood impassively, still watching him. Slowly, it lifted its arm and held out a paw toward him. Blake dropped his own arms, taken aback. The initial survey teams hadn't assigned anywhere near this level of intelligence to the chapaquas. Slowly, he too raised an arm, mimicking the animal's stance. The chapaqua raised its other arm and Blake realized that it held something in its other paw. He peered through the sheets of rain trying to make out what it held. He gasped and got a mouthful of rain for his trouble.

It looked like the chapaqua held a twin of the sample lying back on his desk. It was the right size and shape. Perhaps the chapaqua had got into the environment hut after he had left and taken it.

The chapaqua dropped its paws and scurried back out of view. Blake cursed and scrambled up the slope after it, slipping and sliding over the wet ground, heedless of the mud. He clawed his way over the top lip and glanced from side to side. The flat terrace was empty, and rain splashed in his face. He blinked the water out of his eyes and clambered to his feet. Remaining still, he watched for any further sign of movement, but the chapaqua had well and truly gone.

He wiped as much of the wet leaves and mud from the front of his slicker as he could and entered the cave mouth into still darkness. A glimmer of light ahead showed where the team was. Silence drummed in his ears till the sound of voices reached him from up ahead.

"God, Blake, what happened to you?" said Jen Charlton as he walked into view. Jen was the resident archaeologist on the team.

"You'll never guess what happened, Jen. I just ran into a chapaqua on the trail up here."

"Yeah, well that's unusual," said Cullen with mock surprise.

Blake ignored the engineer. "At first it just stood there. We just stood there looking at each other."

"I know," said Cullen. "It was love at first sight, right?"

Jen cut in. "Look, give it a rest will you, Bill? This might be important. Go on, Blake."

"It was carrying something that looked like that sample I found. Same shape and size anyway. It was gripping it like this." Blake held out his hand to demonstrate. "We knew the chapaquas have opposable digits, but if this thing's a tool .... "

"Sure," said Cullen. "The monkey carries a bit of rock, so now it's a tool user. Sounds like the rain's finally got to you."

"Why don't you shut up and go engineer something, Cullen?"

Cullen just wiped his dirty hands on his coveralls and laughed, but there was no humor in his eyes.

Jen held up her hands. "Come on, Bill. I want to

hear what Blake's got to say." Cullen sniffed, moved over to the wall, and slid down to sit with his back against it, a bored expression on his face.

Blake took a deep breath, resisting the urge to beat the crap out of him. He turned back to Jen. "I don't know what to make of it," he said. "I might have completely the wrong end of things, but maybe those striations are like grips. With all the rain, things are going to be constantly wet, aren't they? So, if you need to use a tool, you're going to need a pretty good gripping surface."

Jen nodded her agreement. "That makes sense." She tugged at one earlobe, thinking. After a moment, she spoke again. "I think you ought to come back here and have a look at this." She turned and stepped into the back of the cave, gesturing over his shoulder for Blake to follow.

The ceiling at the back of the cave dipped down and even Jen had to stoop to enter the small passage leading off into the darkness. Blake tagged along behind, and Cullen, for whatever reason, followed. Blake felt along the walls in almost total darkness, Jen blocking the light in front and Cullen cutting off any illumination from behind. Nothing about the passage was particularly unusual. The entire complex was honeycombed with small passages leading to other caves. They'd been working a section at a time over the last couple of months.

Finally, Jen emerged from the passage mouth and stood in the center of a small chamber. The soft yellow illumination of the portable lighting unit cast crazy shadows over her face. Blake pulled up in front of her, Cullen stepping in to join them. Blake looked around, but it just looked like a cave to him.

"Yes?" he said.

"Look at the floor," said Jen.

Blake stooped down and ran his fingers over the surface, then peered more closely.

"They're tracks," he said. "What do you think made them? The chapaquas?"

"That's my guess," said Jen. "They're the right size.

"It looks like there's been a fair amount of activity. What could the chapaquas want here?"

"But that's not all," she said. "Take a look at this."

Blake stood, cleaned off his hands and stepped over to the wall. It was flatter than the rest. Funny that he hadn't noticed it before. He leaned closer to where Jen pressed her palm flat against the surface. The stone was etched with a gridwork of tiny lines. At the intersection of each set of lines, was a small geometrical shape, clearly edged in the stone. Blake stepped back, his mouth open.

"But—"

"Uh-huh," she said, raising her eyebrows. "Now, how do you think they got there?"

Blake traced the patterns with his fingers.

"My god. These aren't natural."

Jen stepped up beside him. "And look here." Two small slots, barely noticeable in the semi-darkness, marked the patterns at chest height. Their edges were smooth. Blake looked from Jen to Cullen and back again. His mind raced with possibilities. A feeling, almost like hysteria welled up inside him.

"This is..." He laughed. "This is like...contact." He grinned, then shook his head, barely able to believe what he was thinking. "I wonder how old this stuff is. Maybe the chapaquas aren't an evolving life form at all. Maybe they're a degenerate form of an intelligent species." He shook his head again, swept away by the enormity of the thought.

"It could be fairly old," said Cullen, without his usual bravado. "We had to clean off a fair bit of dirt and stuff to get to it."

"Wow." Blake's mind raced. "We've got to get proper lights in here and get some pictures of this." He half-laughed again. "Wow."

"Yeah," said Jen. "We plan to do that in the morning. There's plenty of time."

Blake stepped back, put his hands on his hips and looked at the wall. He didn't care about the rain any more. He barely cared about the sample.

oOo

Two of the small bluish creatures stood there now, barely moving, watching him through the window. Chapaqua activity had really increased around the cave mouth and the huts since they'd discovered the wall. The monkeys were turning up in twos and threes, standing at the edge of the clearing, watching, waiting.

Blake looked up from the pictures of the wall spread out on his desk and out through the sheeting rain at the chapaquas. They didn't move as he pushed his chair back and stood, rubbing at the back of his neck. There must be a link somewhere, but he didn't know what it was. The patterns in the photographs gave him no clue.

He picked up the sample, lifted it to eye level and tilted it back and forward, still rubbing the back of his neck. No clues there either. He lowered his hand and bounced the sample up and down. It was so like a feather, but totally different, and now he knew there was more than one of them. He glanced up at the chapaquas. One held an arm forward, reaching with its paw toward him. Blake frowned, looked down at the sample and back to the small blue-gray creature reaching out across the clearing.

An idea forming in his mind, he lifted the sample and held it up against the window. The other chapaqua lifted its paw now. Both were reaching out to him. The idea took more shape.

Quickly, he turned, crossed to the door, and grabbed his slicker. He pulled it on over his head and stepped outside, the sample still held in his hand. He took three steps into the clearing. The chapaquas still stood watching. He held out the sample, making sure they could see it. Both raised their paws toward him. Blake stepped forward, expecting the chapaquas to take off into the trees as they normally did, but this time they stayed. He took two more steps across the clearing. Both faces looked up at him expectantly.

Blake crossed the final distance between them and stood, the rain pounding on the top of his head. The chapaquas were just under the start of the canopy and had some shelter. The one standing to the left held out its paw. It was the same one that he'd met on the path, he was sure. Blake shrugged and held out his own hand imitating its stance. The chapaqua dropped its paw. Blake frowned. He had thought for a moment he was making headway. The one on the right held up its paw this time, and in it sat the duplicate of his sample. He had been right. Blake lifted his other arm—the one holding the sample.

The first chapaqua leapt. It crossed the three strides between them almost faster than Blake could see and wrapped itself around his outstretched arm. Blake staggered backward, tripped, and landed in a pool of water, his passenger still firmly wrapped around his arm. The other chapaqua raced forward, leaned down, wrested the sample from his hand and took off into the undergrowth. The first chapaqua, using its hind legs, launched itself from Blake's chest and raced off after its companion.

Blake cursed and scrambled to his feet, slipping in the mud. How could he have been so stupid? Both chapaquas had gone and his sample had gone with them. There wasn't a hope in hell of finding them in the trees, but he had to try. He broke into a run and raced into the trees along the well-used path. That had been the direction they had taken—the same place he had first seen the chapaqua holding the sample.

He patted at his pockets as he staggered up the path. Estrella was going to kill him. He'd walked outside without his locator again—probably just as well under the circumstances. Slowing his pace to a jog, he listened through the rain noise, straining to hear any sound of movement around him.

By the time he reached the end of the path, he was out of breath and despairing. He stood at the base of the last rise, his hands on his hips, trying to regain his breath. A rustling to the side of him made him turn his head and a chapaqua bounded up the slope right past him. A moment later, another passed him on the other side, then another. What the hell was going on?

Blake took a step upward toward the lip, intent on his footing. When he looked up again, a small blue-gray face was watching him with wide yellow eyes. Blake stepped again, and the face was joined by another. One more step, and both chapaquas moved to the end of the path, blocking his way. He could see up over the edge now. Behind the two standing in his way, was a steady stream of chapaquas. They came from all directions and filed into the cave mouth. A couple of them glanced in his direction as they passed.

As he took his next step, the first chapaqua held out its paw, palm toward him. The meaning was clear. Blake was to stay where he was. He shook his head and took another step. The chapaqua gestured again. It clearly wanted him to stop, but Blake wasn't having any of it. Something was going on in the caves and he was going to find out what.

He reached the top of the path, drawing level with the two chapaquas. One turned its head to its companion, looked back at Blake and shoved him gently in the chest.

"What?" said Blake, barely able to believe what it had just done. He made to step forward. The chapaqua reached forward and shoved him firmly in the middle of the chest.

The force was enough to send Blake's feet out from under him. He slid and slithered back down the path, bumping against rocks, scrabbling for purchase while leaves and trees whipped past him on either side. He slid to a halt on his back, staring up at purple-black clouds, with a fountain of water tumbling into his eyes and mouth. Ignoring the hurt, he turned and pushed himself to his feet.

A clear muddy track showed where he had careened down the slope. He followed it to the top, but there was no sign of the chapaquas. He cursed, and, taking a deep breath, headed back up.

Halfway up, the ground started to shake. He felt the vibration through his boots and threw out a hand to steady himself. The vibration grew to a rumble, and the rumble became a roar that filled the air. Blake fell to his knees and looked up. The noise came from above him, in the direction of the caves.

Ponderously, a section of the mountain where the caves should have been, detached itself and rose slowly into the air. Pieces of earth and vegetation tumbled from its sides. Rocks the size of boulders fell, turning in the air as they plummeted. A whole vast chunk of the terrain lifted into the air and slowly headed for the clouds. With it went the roaring, fading higher and higher into the sky.

Blake sat on his hands and knees, the rain beating down around him, his mouth open, staring at the sky. Gradually, his hearing returned, the ringing in his ears replaced by the sound of droplets against his head.

oOo

Estrella, Jen, and Cullen found him sitting on the path, staring into his hands, and shaking his head.

"Blake, what happened?" said Estrella, crouching down in front of him. She reached out a hand to his shoulder. "When we heard the noise, and we realized you didn't have your locator with you, we came looking. Are you okay?"

Blake looked up into her eyes and laughed. "Yeah, I'm okay."

"So, what happened up here?"

"Hubris, 'Strell. That's what happened." He laughed again.

"What do you mean, Blake?" asked Jen. "You're not making any sense."

"Hubris. We couldn't see it. Too bound up in our own self-importance.... They're gone."

"Who's gone?" said Jen with a frown.

"The chapaquas. Gone." Blake waved vaguely up the path behind him. "We had contact all right. We thought we were watching them. Cute little proto primates. Developing life forms out near Centauri. They were watching us. The chapaquas I mean. We got too close, I guess. Saw too much and they came and took away the evidence, and now they're gone. I wonder where to. I wonder how far *they* came." Blake shook his head again and chuckled.

"Blake, what the hell are you going on about?" asked Cullen.

"Up there, Engineer. See for yourself."

Cullen shrugged and climbed up the rest of the path. His curse when he reached the top was loud and clear even above the sound of the rain.

"Well, at least they didn't get the photographs of the cave wall. That's something. Not half as good as intelligent monkeys, but...." Blake shrugged and gave a short laugh, leaning back with his face up to the rain.

-The End-

The Bodysnatchin' Man

The Sheriff came a-huntin' for the Bodysnatchin' Man. He came down to Snake Eyes in his nice clean suit with his magic cane and his goons and he come looking. He came right on down to Mud Town. We saw him coming, the Bodysnatchin' Man and me, and we knew what he was after.

So, Little Sister, you listen up good, cause I got me a tale to tell about the Bodysnatchin' Man and how I come to know him.

Now me, I been maybe thirteen, fourteen, then. Been doing little things like the 'lectrics, but mainly I been a righteous whore, making me a little bit of money for the gas and things. The Bodysnatchin' Man—oh my, but he was pretty—he was maybe fifteen. We come together and right away I noticed that his skin was smooth. He didn't have none of the rashes and sores all over his body like normal people. His legs, they was smooth like steel. He had a mop of thick brown hair, and his eyes, well they was green. He had mud smeared on his face and on his clothes, but so did most folk then. Back then the floods were real bad. Everywhere was mud.

It was one heavy day just like this one when I met the Bodysnatchin' Man. He was young and sweet and fine, and through no fault of his own, when he come to me, he was running from the police.

Our people, we had our camp woven in the shadow of the old big ship down in Snake Eyes. Me, I was doing a good line of whoring, working from my reed house built hard up against the big ship. I been doing good business too, cause the ship kind of drew folk to it. The police pretty much left us alone down there. They kept right away from Mud Town. You wouldn't remember none of that, cause you was just a baby then. There were tracks leading in and out of that place, from every which way, and the Bodysnatchin' Man just come walking in. He walks right up to me, and he looks me in the eye. I never knew why it was me out of all people he come up to.

"You've got to help me," he says, in that nice fine voice of his.

I looked him up and down. He's not the sort that belongs in Mud Town and I told him so. He explains that he's on the run, that he come to Mud Town cause he was knowing that the police stay away from the place. He tells me he comes from the City, that he was City folk.

Well I could tell right away that he was City folk—him all fine and smooth like that. But I couldn't understand what he was doing on the run. City folk like him, they don't get trouble with the police. So I asks him.

"What you done?" I say.

Well, you know what he tells me? He tells me he done run over someone with his skimmer, and instead of leaving him there to lie, he takes this boy to a med centre right out on the edges of the suburbs to get him fixed. Him coming from the City and all, he doesn't understand that ain't the way folks do things down in Snake Eyes. He couldn't be knowing about the Sheriff and his needs.

Now I remember the Sheriff back then. That Sheriff, he was a tall man. All full and twisted with hate he was. He had a big white hat and a squint in his right eye, and he was always carrying a cane. He almost never got out of his skimmer, cause of his bad hip. That's the reason all this trouble started. The Sheriff'd just sit there and yell and shout and order his men about to do his say-so – ordered near everybody about.

Now, that cane of his was special. Up near the top it had this clear place, filled with some sort of milky stuff. Folks said he could use that cane and shoot you full of that stuff. Make you like dead, but still alive, it would. That was for the parts. Keep them fresh, so they said.

When the Bodysnatchin' Man came to me and told me what he did, I knew right then and there. That boy he knocked down in his skimmer was going to be the Sheriff's new hip and the Sheriff was out for blood. He wanted the Bodysnatchin'

Man to make recompense. The Sheriff figured that the Bodysnatchin' Man was going to be the hip instead. He figured that since the Bodysnatchin' Man had taken his new hip to a med centre, instead of letting him lie, that he was going to take the Bodysnatchin' Man in that boy's place.

When we saw them coming—you get plenty a warning down here in Mud Town —I grabbed hold of his clean smooth arm and we lit on out of there. The Sheriff and his boys, they didn't know we'd gone, didn't know the Bodysnatchin' Man was with me. They just knew he was somewhere in Mud Town, so they near tore the place apart, going from house to house, slopping through the mud. But me, I was smart. When we took off out of there, I kept real close to the side of the ship so's we'd blend in. What with the mud and all, we kept low, and wove in and out of the reeds and stuff, and we blended in real good. Took the Sheriff and his boys some time to cotton on to the Bodysnatchin' Man not being there, and that gave us time to get away before they came after us.

While we was running, low and fast, I asks him his name. He wasn't called the Bodysnatchin' Man back then. That came later, by other folks, after they found out what he'd done.

"Kevin," he tells me.

Kevin. Now that was an old style name —the sort still used by City folk. We didn't have no names like that. We all used names like Wolf, and

Dirtdog and stuff. So Kevin, I knew he was truly from the City, with a name like that. He looks at me as we're running low, and he tell me he doesn't understand what he's done. He asks me why I was helping him and though I couldn't really figure it out myself, I told him.

"Kevin," I says to him. "Folks like you got no place being down in Mud Town. Sides, I like the look of you."

And I did. He was so fine and pretty. I just wanted a piece of him then and there.

Anyways, we lit on out, with the Sheriff's men not far behind. We slipped our way through the outskirts of Mud Town, getting further and further away, with the smell of the swamp all ripe and rich in our nostrils. I had it in mind to get him right away from there, get him back to the City where the Sheriff and his men couldn't touch him. It would've been such a shame to have one as pretty as him just wasted to give that mean old Sheriff a new part. Just wasn't right.

After a time, we came out of the mud flats and got into the open ground. You get all trees and things out there, and then there starts the houses. Now Kevin was tired, but we had to keep on going, cause I knew if we stopped the Sheriff would catch us up and that'd be that. And I'd be going along for the ride, seeing as I'd been helping him to get away. I knew then and there that we weren't going to make it without some help, so I starts looking for a faster way to get us out of there.

When you come out of Mud Town and you're still in Snake Eyes, things change the more you get away from the ship. They got proper houses and things out there, not like the ones we got in Mud Town. Well I was looking hard for a way we could get away real quick. I knew it wasn't going to be long before the Sheriff and his goons would be high-tailing it after us.

You got to understand here, Little Sister, I don't hold with taking those things that don't belong to you—now that ain't right, doing that—but we didn't have much of a choice. So I look around. There's plenty of houses thereabouts, like it's just starting on to being right at the edges of the City. It's still Snake Eyes kind of, but it's kind of not as well. Anyways, I sees a place that has a skimmer parked outside. Me being good with the 'lectrics, I got me the idea that just maybe I could get into this skimmer and get it started. I didn't need to drive it; the Bodysnatchin' Man could do that. I didn't have no need of knowing how to drive.

Sure enough, it was easy to get into that thing—just got some simple codes on the door. Kevin, he stood there, keeping watch, making sure no one came out and saw us. Took me a little while to work out how it got started, my heart pounding in my chest all the way, but once I did, we was out of there. The skimmer was old and beat up, but it worked. So we were in that skimmer and gone.

Simple as that.

I turn to Kevin, and I tell him, "Head for the City."

"But what about you?" he says to me.

I tell him I'm coming with him to make sure he's going to be all right. He doesn't understand the ways of Snake Eyes, and without me along to help him out, he's just going to find himself in more trouble than when he started.

This skimmer we took, well despite it being a bit old, a bit beat up, it's one of those small, fast jobs. Does just the trick. Cause it ain't got too much weight, it's easy for it to climb them mud hills without falling over or sinking into the slush like the big ones do. He nods his head and starts her up and we slide on out of that place. Cause that skimmer's so light, it doesn't even leave a proper trail behind in the mud and grass and stuff.

While we was floating along, I was keeping one eye on the way we was going on the other on the Bodysnatchin' Man. I could feel myself aching to have him, he was so fine, but there was no place or time for that then. The mud's all whipping by below us and we've got the police there hot on our tail. No time for anything but running.

Wasn't long before we heard the Sheriff and his men chasing along behind, sirens blaring. Though we couldn't see them yet, Kevin, he starts to panic, but I tell him it's going to be all right. I talk to him like I talk to one of the guys who comes to see me with problems of his own. All nice and gentle. I got plenty of practice at that. Well, that seems to work all right, cause he starts paying attention to the driving and not to them police that are following along behind.

I don't know too much about those places outside Mud Town, but I know enough to point us in the right direction. I tell Kevin to keep on driving, up through the hills and away. Somewhere we got to find a place to hole up, where the Sheriff ain't going to find us, cause if we keep straight on going, they're going to catch us in the open. Those big old police skimmers, well they move too fast for us to get away once we're out of Snake Eyes and in the clear. Kevin sees the sense of what I'm telling him, and he keeps on driving, right the way I tell him, never taking his eyes off the way ahead.

We travel for maybe an hour, uphill and through the mud rivers, keeping to the channels so's we'd be harder to follow. No matter what we did though, those police skimmers, they kept coming on after us. Finally, I decide the only thing we got to do is hide, so I start looking out for somewhere we can lay low 'til the heat dies down. Sure enough, before long, atop one of those big old hills you see out on the edges of the City, I see an old wooden house. It looks like there ain't been nobody there for ages. There's big old trees up there with vines all hanging from the branches, and there's bushes all thick and tangled all around it, so

I nudge Kevin and points him to head that way.

This big old house has so much stuff all about, I think it's just the thing for us. We can hide the skimmer in the bushes and lay low inside for a while. At least until the police move off to look somewhere else. So, that's exactly what we do. Kevin drives the skimmer up the hill, and we jump out and drag all sorts of branches and leaves and stuff and cover up that skimmer real good. Then we slip inside through a broken door into the house.

I was right, cause there ain't been anyone in this house for months, maybe years, or so it seems. The walls, they're starting to fall down and there's gaps in the roof. All the wood's got thick green moss all over, and you can see the wet black poking through underneath. I don't mind too much. It ain't much different from living in an old reed house down in Mud Town. I could see by Kevin's face that he didn't think much of it, but I told him, "You ain't got much choice."

He nodded to me, cause he could see the sense of what I was saying. We looked out through the walls and the windows. Right up high there on the hill, we had a view for miles around. We could see the big old wooden houses thereabouts and we could see the hills and the valleys clear across to the ship. We could even pick out Mud Town from there.

Happens we were just in time. The Sheriff's

men were coming close in them skimmers of theirs, and Kevin and me, we lay down on the floor, hiding in the shadows, peering out through the cracks in the walls and just praying that the Sheriff's men were going to pass us by. Cause of the way I told Kevin to go, and cause of that skimmer we had, we'd left no real tracks behind us. The grasses were already springing back like we'd never even been there, so I was thinking maybe we had a chance. I was hoping none of them saw the place where Kevin drove the skimmer through the bushes, though I thought we covered it up real good.

We waited there, him and me, lying flat on the damp, hard wood floor, watching and waiting, the smell of moss all strong in our faces. My mouth was real dry, and I could hear my heart banging real loud in my ears, making like my chest was going to burst. The police skimmers, they hung around for what seemed to be hours and hours. I thought maybe I was going to die of fear when this big old skimmer stops at the bottom of the hill and the Sheriff steps out. He stands there in his big white hat, poking the ground with his cane and looking all around. I saw him look up at the house, and stare at it for a long time, but then one of his goons calls something to him and he turns away. I'd been holding my breath by then, but finally he gets back into his skimmer, and it takes off and he's gone. The other skimmers hang around for a while, search all over the place, but then finally they go too, and I feel like I can breathe again.

I wanted to make sure they was well clear before we took our skimmer out and headed for the City, so I decide we got to wait there for a time. While we was lying there, I take hold of Kevin's hand and I press it tight. Eventually it started to get dark.

Now, ever since he came up to me, I been wanting this boy. So, I'm lying there in the dark, holding his hand and he turns and looks at me. He's lying there in the darkness just watching me and holding on to my hand. Right about then I just couldn't help myself. I reach up and take hold of his head and I kiss him hard against his mouth. Well that was that. Wasn't long before we were rushing to get our clothes off and be with each other. It was just so fine with his naked body lying next to mine —his smooth clear skin pressing up against me and his firm young muscles moving slow and sweet. Three times we did it, one after the other, and then again in the morning with the smell of each other strong and rich all around us. He even smelled sweet, that boy.

About mid-morning, we finally decided we had to get going. He was kind of sheepish pulling on his clothes, and that was sort of sweet too. Well, we checked, but there was no sign of the police. The way was clear. We pulled the skimmer out from under them branches and headed off towards the City. All the way, we didn't see one police skimmer, so I figured the Sheriff must have given it up. But all the way, Kevin was kind of watching me out of the corner of his eye.

We got to the edge of the City about midday. Out there, on the edge of the City I told him to stop. I knew I couldn't go no further. My place was back in Snake Eyes, down in Mud Town. I knew there wasn't no place for me in the City. So he stops and I get out of the skimmer.

"What are you doing?" he asks me, so I tell him.

"I gotta go now, Kevin," I say.

I leave him there at the edge of the City and I say my good-byes. He tells me I should stay, that he'll look after me, but I knows that ain't right. There wasn't no place for me in the City. That was his place. He looks at me long and hard, but I just turn around and walk away, though it's hurting me inside to do it.

That was the last I saw of the Bodysnatchin' Man. I never did see him again, not once. But he done left something with me —something sure as fine as he was.

Now you have to know this, Little Sister, cause I'm getting old. I'm nearly thirty years now and my time's going to be coming soon. When I'm gone, you're going to have to look after my boy and take care of him real good.

You can tell, you look at him real close, he

ain't the same as most folk down here in Mud Town. You see how smooth his skin is? Smooth like steel. That boy's strong and proud, and he's going to be the father of many a child down here in Snake Eyes. The women, they're going to love him, that's for sure. You got to understand that has to be the way. You got to make sure that boy has his way with as many women as is willing to love him.

Well, that's how it was. The Bodysnatchin' Man, though he didn't know it, left us *all* a little something. Sure as I'm telling you this, one day what he left is going to help us. I ain't saying it will for sure, but maybe that something will help us *all* climb right back out of this here mud.

-The End-

The Greening

There had been little warning and by the time they knew, it was too late. Schuman Kransfield smacked into the northern reaches of the Siberian wastes and humanity breathed a collective sigh of relief. The rogue comet had missed anywhere that mattered. There were repercussions, of course, but none as severe as if it had landed in a centre of population.

Then the deaths began.

At first, no one linked the disease with the comet. Gradually, as the plague spread and they traced its origins, the realisation came. Schuman Kransfield had carried a passenger through the far reaches of space. Once on Earth, travel was quick and easy.

It caught a train to Moscow. From there, it boarded a plane to Frankfurt. Once in Frankfurt, it was just a short hop to most of the other population centres in the world.

oOo

Row upon even row of green-striped sun lounges stretched across the park. Warm, clean sunlight filtered down from above. It filled his limbs with strength and energy. Somewhere, kids yelled and laughed. They dashed between the rows of people relaxing, chasing each other in and out of the sun lounges. Simon turned his head, seeking out the noise and muttered at the disturbance.

Eaters thought Simon. *It could only be Eaters*. No

sensible Photo kid would be wasting this time of day. He turned lazily to the side, first one way, then the other, seeing if he could catch sight of them. It appeared they'd run off for now, somewhere out of the park and away. He stretched languorously, exposing another part of his skin to the sun's remaining nourishing rays. It was at times like this that he wondered why they just couldn't pack all the Eaters up and send them away somewhere.

Eaters—they were supposed to be just like him, but he couldn't help shuddering. Just because they were supposed to be people, didn't mean he had to think of them as the same. From time to time Simon wondered what it was like in the Plague Years — not that he could remember those times. Maybe if he could, he'd be able to find a bit more sympathy, or maybe he'd just end up hating them more.

Millions had died of the mystery disease back then. Some were immune; some had survived. The survivors had been left with the legacy they passed on from generation to generation and now it lived within them all. The others, the immunes, had become the Eaters.

The sun glided past the tree line at the park's edge, splitting the light into shafts that dappled the broad open spaces. He sat up and yawned. All around him, others were sitting or getting to their feet. He leaned down, snagged his shirt, and pulled it on as he stood. While he slipped into his trousers, he scanned the periphery, searching for any further sign of the Eater kids, but they were well and truly gone. They'd be off somewhere now, no doubt preparing for their *dinner*. He gave an involuntary shudder. Horrible, pink-skinned creatures shovelling food into their mouths: it wasn't a pretty thought.

The park's other occupants were drifting off in ones and twos, heading off to their families or jobs. Simon made a mental note to pick up some supplements on the way to work; supplies had been getting short since the start of the Eater action. The slow-down on production wouldn't hurt him personally, not yet. He had a supply of Nutri-Grow direct from the production line. He'd be fine. But he still needed some other stuff.

Who did the Eaters think they were anyway trying to hold everyone to ransom? It wouldn't do them any good. Maybe that's what things had been like back in the dim dark days of the racial equality movement before the Plague had changed everyone's life. People had the solution then, but sadly, the Eaters didn't have a home they could be shipped back to. They were everywhere, damn them.

Simon shook his head and walked slowly from the park. It would be dark soon, and he didn't want to be late—not with the current problems brewing.

oOo

Schuman Kransfield Disease, or SKD, as it came to be known, swept across the globe. Its appearance was rapid and devastating. Through Africa, it moved more slowly, but the results were the same. People died in droves. Some survived. Some were immune, though the immunes were few and far between.

They tried treating it a number of ways. None of the solutions worked. When the survivors started turning green, they tried to treat that as well.

Then the survivors stopped eating.

oOo

Simon stood on the street and stared up at the glass and metal edifice of his office building. All around him, the street was full of other Photos arriving for work. Elsewhere in the city, the Eaters would be going about their business, preparing for nights in front of their televisions, or congregating in bars. Then they would sleep, while the real people got on with their lives. He grimaced and made for the front doors. He had a life to get on with too.

He nodded as he passed security and headed for the elevator. They were waiting for him when he walked inside.

"We're down to 75% already," said Cosgrove, before Simon even had time to put down his things.

"At least give me the time to get in the door," said Simon. The panic was starting already. Bill Cosgrove, normally level headed and calm, looked worried. A deep frown was etched upon his big square face. Simon dropped his belongings on the desk and turned to face Cosgrove. "We can survive on that, can't we?" he asked.

"Sure, but if it drops any lower...." said Cosgrove.

"Yes, yes. I know," said Simon. "It's not getting any better. Have you seen it? Panic buying's already started on the supplements. I tried to pick some up on the way in. Not a hope. Carla, have we received their latest demands?"

Carla Matheson nodded from the corner. "They're

unchanged. They want double overtime and a 10% raise on basic."

"Who the hell do they think they are?" muttered Cosgrove. "Bloody Foodies."

Simon pulled out his chair and sat. "Bill, unless you're prepared to go and slave away on the production line yourself, unless we all are, then they can do what they damn well like. I don't think we should put up with it any more than you do, but unless we can come to some sort of agreement, they've got us where they want us. You know what they're like." He ran his fingers through his hair and sighed. "No sensible Photo is going to work the factories, are they? So, we've got no option. Have we done the sums? Can we afford what they want?"

"Not a chance," said Carla. "It'd send us broke within half a year."

"Oh, great. The Board is going to love this," said Simon. He turned to look out over the darkening city. *What next?* he thought. He held out his hands, palms down to the desk and stared at the green-tinged skin. And it was his place to work out the solution. Just great!

"Right, we're going to have to set up a meet," he said. "Who's their spokesperson?"

"Some guy called Marcus Hall. He's pretty hard-line by the sounds of him. I don't like your chances. He's your typical Foodie. You know the sort," said Cosgrove.

Simon grimaced and nodded. "Well, what can we give them? No ... scratch that. What can we *afford* to give them?"

"Um...looking at the figures," said Carla, "we might get away with 5% at most and time and a half on overtime, but that would be stretching it."

Simon manoeuvred past his chair back and walked over to her corner. The slight purple light of the grow lamp perched over her desk tinged her face with blue-white. "Show me," he said. She handed him the papers and he walked back over to the window. He stared down at the figures, verifying what she had said. She was right; any more would be really pushing it.

He sucked in his cheeks and looked out across the skyline, thinking what he could get away with.

"Right, we'll offer them two and a half. Bill, go ahead and set up a meeting."

oOo

Initial efforts concentrated on isolating the invader. It was identified as a new virus. Then came the realisation that those who survived were infected with something new — chloroplasts. The finding was met with disbelief. After more tests, the result was undeniable. Some bright researcher remembered experiments that had treated primitive plants with antibiotics in an effort to prove that chloroplasts were originally the result of an infectious symbiotic agent. The disbelief was replaced by guarded acceptance. The teams were running out of options. As a last desperate measure, they tried it. It worked remarkably well, except for one problem—the subjects died. The chloroplasts were gone, but the cure had killed the afflicted. Slowly people started to realise; the Photosynthetics were among us.

One by one, we fell.

oOo

Simon sat at the boardroom table, playing with his pen. A sheaf of papers lay before him. They'd met the Eaters half way, organised the meeting for three in the afternoon. It was cutting into valuable sun time, but it would be worth it if they could reach some sort of compromise. Carla sat beside him, her recorder in front of her.

"What's keeping them?" she asked.

"Would you expect anything more from Eaters," said Simon. "They'll be here. You didn't really believe they'd be on time, did you?"

She gave a wry snort.

There was a knock on the door, and the Eater representatives were ushered into the room. Marcus Hall took the lead. Simon recognised him from his picture in the company files. He wore stained blue overalls, the company logo on the breast pocket. Simon didn't recognise his two companions.

Hall was a heavy-set man with a ruddy complexion. Sandy hair was cropped short on his bullet-shaped head. He carried a stack of folders under one arm. The others, Foodies both, stood a little behind him. One was a short black man, the other older and greying. He had an unhealthy pallor about his fleshy pink face. Simon swallowed back his feelings and forced a smile as he stood.

"Gentlemen, please." He indicated the chairs on the opposite side of the table. "I'm so glad you agreed to meet with us at such short notice. Please, take a seat and we can get things underway. Now, would you like anything to, um ... drink, before we get started." All three shook their heads. Hall took the lead, dumped the stack of folders on the table, and pulled out a chair. The others sat on either side of him, crossing their arms in front of them. Hall spoke first.

"Right, let's get down to it, Leary. We all know what the deal is. Is the company going to meet our demands or not?"

"Now, let's slow things down a bit can we, Marcus—if I can call you Marcus? We need to discuss the options here. You have to understand; it's a question of economics. The company appreciates all the hard work you men put in, but there's the bottom line to think of."

Hall sat back, his hands flat upon the table. "Cut the crap, Leary. I don't need to hear your company garbage. Just tell us what we want to know."

Simon could see this wasn't going to be easy.

"All right ... the company has carefully considered your proposal. And after lengthy analysis of the operating costs, and productivity, we have found your demands to be a little, shall we say, unreasonable?" Hall snorted and moved to pick up his folders. Simon quickly raised a placating hand. "But wait, please. Hear me out. The company is prepared to make a counter-offer—one that we think is very reasonable under the circumstances. And we really hope that you'll agree with the fairness of our proposal."

Hall glowered at him across the table and crossed his arms. "I'm listening," he said. Simon glanced at Carla before continuing. This was it.

"The company is able to offer two per cent. We will be stretching our capabilities at that much."

Before he could continue, Hall growled something unintelligible, angrily picked up his folders and shook his head. He motioned to his two companions who also stood, hostility written across their faces.

"No way, Leary," said Hall. "You'll be humming a different tune when your precious supplements dry up." He stalked from the room with his companions in tow, slamming the door behind them.

oOo

Within the space of a few short years, everything changed. Famine became a thing of the past. Africa and the Indian Subcontinent clambered free from their hand-to-mouth existence, and they thrived. Populations, stripped of their numbers by the Plague Years became re-established, and the equatorial regions grew strong and healthy. Then came the polarisation between the infected and the immune—the hiving off of Eater and Photo into their separate strands. No longer did the world have many races: it now had two.

oOo

Simon sat nervously in the President's outer office. The secretary glanced at him a couple of times, but was more intent upon her keyboard. He wondered how much she knew. A full twenty minutes he sat, counting out the President's displeasure in seconds.

"Mr. Klein will see you now," she said finally.

Klein was standing by the window looking out over the darkened city when Simon entered. Subtle lighting tinged the office with purple and blue. Simon stood and waited. Finally, he cleared his throat.

"What's the story, Leary?" said the President without turning. "I thought I could trust you to settle this."

Simon gave an involuntary swallow. "I know, Sir. The food-shovel—um, Eaters weren't there for reasoned negotiation. They were there to make a point."

Klein swung to face him. "I don't care why they were there. It was up to you to fix it. I was relying on you, Leary. Now, what are you going to do? No, not what are you going to do. What are you *doing?"*

"Our only option, Sir, is to try and set up another meeting. I suspect that it's not going to be that easy. But unless we can come to some agreement soon, the company is going to start hurting."

"And we don't want that, Leary, do we? I'm giving you to the end of the week to get this thing resolved. If you can't come up with something by then...." Klein turned back to the window, his implication lying heavy in the air.

As he left the secretary's office, his mind was cataloguing and rejecting options one after the other. If Klein thought there was any possibility they could reach a compromise by week's end, he was crazy. "Dammit," he breathed to himself. He was going to have to find another way.

oOo

Integration was the first thought, but the living patterns of the two strands were so different. Photos lay in the sun during the day, recharging their bodily stores. Their social interaction became different. No longer were there dinner parties, or going out to grab a bite to eat. The developed an abhorrence of many things which had, until a few years before, been natural parts of day to day existence. Photo suburbs arose, then gradually, a whole new way of life. As the infection passed from generation to generation, the numbers grew.

In the colder, more northern climes, the Photos started to take supplements to counter the lack of sunlight. There was vast migration to the equatorial regions, but others chose to stay. Centres of population, finance and industry gravitated to those regions best suited climatically. Not only was there a societal shift, but a geographical shift as well. Vast agricultural belts diminished in size, only having to produce enough to satisfy the Eaters. The farms were run by Eaters. Distribution was run by Eaters. And slowly, there appeared Eater shops, and Eater schools and Eater towns. Crossover appeared in those areas where daytime activities, or those means of production more suited to the Eater population matched the needs of the Photos.

oOo

Short of violence, what Simon was considering seemed the most likely solution. He went through personnel and found all he could on the man, Marcus Hall. Hall lived in a downmarket Eater suburb. A wife, two kids, all the normal stuff. No criminal record or disciplinary problems during his history with the company. He'd been with Justin Klein Maglock for fifteen years, working the factory floor. So, what was it now that had suddenly made him so vocal? Until a month ago, there had been agitators, but Hall was not among them. Was it something to do with the family? He pored over the file, but it was not enough. He had to get to know the man. Then he'd burn the bastard. He smiled wryly.

Steeling himself for the charade, he stretched for the phone.

A rather dumpy Eater woman answered. She wore an apron and dark hair sat haphazardly atop her head.

"Yes?" she said, looking confused. The sound of kids fighting came from the background. She turned and gave a strident yell over one shoulder. "Pipe down in there!" Then she turned back to face the screen, adjusting a strand of hair. "Sorry, um, can I help you?"

"Yes, I'd like to speak to Marcus please."

A frown flickered across her face.

"And you are?"

"Simon Leary, Head of Employee Relations for JKM."

"Just a minute." She disappeared from the screen. Her voice drifted through from the other room. "There's a Greenie on the phone, Mark. Says his name's Cleary or something, from the company. You want to take it?"

A moment later, Hall wandered into the room. He still had on his company overalls, and he was chewing. Simon swallowed back his distaste and slipped on his practised smile.

"Yeah, Leary. What do you want? We're in the

middle of dinner."

"I'm sorry for disturbing you, Marcus, but I think we need to talk."

"Talk about what? We did all our talking." He reached to cut the connection.

"No, wait! Just hear me out will you, Hall? We need to talk. Seriously, the situation is not quite that simple. Is there somewhere we can meet...in private."

Hall's face echoed his suspicion. He checked back over his shoulder, then leaned closer to the screen. "What game are you playing here, Leary. You think I'm some sort of idiot?"

"No game. Listen, the company's not as strong as you might think. I can't talk about it over the phone. We have to meet."

Hall frowned. He had stopped chewing. After a long pause, he finally spoke. "Yeah, well...maybe if you came here. I can't be seen talking to you. If you can get to my place without being seen...."

"Your place? Isn't there somewhere else?"

"Too many questions. I tell you, Leary, this better be good."

"Oh, believe me, it will be. Tonight? I'll see if I can get there just after midnight. How's that?"

Hall nodded. He reached forward, still frowning and cut the connection.

Simon sat back from the screen and thought. It had been far easier than he'd expected. Good. Tonight it was. And after all, every man had his price.

oOo

Simon pulled into the drive and cut the power. The streets were dead. A window further down the row of suburban houses glowed with light, but most of the places were dark. He sat staring at Hall's house, his lips pressed tightly together. What the hell was he doing here? Still, there was a job to do, so he'd better get to it. He opened the door and stepped out, closing it as quietly as he could behind him. Klein had better appreciate what he was about to do.

He stood waiting nervously on the porch, waiting for someone to answer. Hall himself finally came to the door and ushered him quickly inside, glancing out to make sure they hadn't been seen.

"Right," said Hall. "What's so important that you had to come here? I've asked you into my home. The least you can do is be straight with me, Leary."

Simon looked around. They stood in a hallway. Coats hung on a rack near the door. Pictures graced the walls.

"Look, can we go and sit somewhere?" said Simon.

Hall rubbed his hand over the top of his head, hesitated, and then seemed to make up his mind. "Yeah, all right," he said. "Follow me." He led the way into a living room that was little different from any suburban house. If Simon didn't know better, it could easily have belonged to a Photo. There were pictures of Hall's kids on the mantle, a games console in the corner — one of the cheaper sort — and ornaments and flowers and anything he'd expect to find in anybody's home. The only thing missing was the faint purple glow. Hall motioned him to a chair and sat himself.

"I won't offer you a drink," Hall said. "I know your type don't. But maybe some water."

Simon shook his head as he took the offered seat. "Look, Marcus," he said. "I know it's difficult and I thank you for agreeing to see me. I'm just trying to work out what's happening is all. You've a good record with the company. Not a hint of trouble, but now you seem prepared to jeopardise all that — for what? There's more going on here than a few lousy per cent in a pay packet. Tell me there's not."

"What is this, Leary? Some kind of threat? 'Cause if it is..."

Simon lifted a hand. "No, no. I'm not here to threaten you. I'm just trying to understand, that's all. Perhaps we can work out what it is you need. The company may not be in a position to meet the demands, but surely you *personally* have needs, if you see what I'm saying...?"

Hall rubbed his hand over the top of his head again and looked away. He brought his hands back in front of his face and cupped them in front of his mouth. He sighed, then looked at Simon over the tops of his fingers, a long hard look. "You and me, were not so different, are we Leary?" he asked.

"No, of course not." Hall's response had caught him off guard, but the response came automatically.

Hall was still looking at him intently. "Well, why should things be any different for us? Look at this place. You got kids Leary?" Simon shook his head. Hall gave a knowing nod then proceeded to crack his knuckles. "Well, if you did, you might know what I mean. You think you can come here and simply *buy* me?"

"I don't see—"

"You look at your kids and you see the future. That's what it's all about. That's what I'm talking about. I want better things for my kids. I want more than I can give them while all you Greenie bastards are keeping us down. There shouldn't have to be different rules."

Simon stood and walked to the mantle, looked at the pictures lined across the top. "These them?" he asked ignoring the blatant slur.

"Yeah," he said with a sigh. "That's Jessie, the oldest and Katrina."

Simon turned and looked down at Hall. Sometimes he wondered what it would be like to have children, but getting all paternal wasn't going to help the current problem. He had to at least appear sympathetic. "Good looking kids."

"Right. Look Leary, you're here now. Say what you've come to say. Spell it out. I'm listening."

Simon walked back to the chair and sat. Hall was watching him sceptically, but there was still that intensity in his eyes. "Marcus, what I started to tell you in the meetings is true. The company can't meet the demands your people are making. What I offered was as much as the company can afford. However, if you cooperate, if you can swing the others around to accepting the offer, I'm sure we can make it worth your while. The others listen to you."

At that moment, a voice came from the hall outside. "Daddy, is that you? I heard voices. I can't sleep. I want a drink of water."

"Go back to bed, Trina. Daddy's busy."

"But I'm thirsty."

"Go and ask your mother."

"No, I want you to get it."

Before Hall was out of the chair, his little girl had walked into the room. Hall tried quickly to stand in the way, to block Simon's view, but he was too late. Something was different about the child as she looked at him with wide brown eyes. She looked somehow different from the picture on the mantle. Then Simon realised what it was—the girl's skin was tinged vaguely green.

Simon looked in disbelief. Making sure he wasn't imagining it, he frowned, then sat back stunned. Hall looked guiltily at him over his shoulder, then quickly ushered the child from the room.

What did it mean? How could an Eater kid be showing green? Unless...

What had Hall said? "You look at your kids and you see the future."

It was some minutes before Hall returned, and when he did, he walked very slowly into the room. "You saw, right?" he said in a quiet voice.

Simon nodded, not knowing what to say. But here was his tool. He could use this. When word got out among his fellow workers....

Hall slumped into the chair. "It started about a month ago. Only the girl. It hasn't touched the boy at all. I don't know what we're going to do." He stared blankly in front of him. "Maybe this is the start of something, maybe it's not. I don't know." There was a pause, and then he seemed to regain focus. "I guess it's some sort of mutation. I've looked in the books. I know what happened in history. We try to treat what she's got and...." He shrugged. "We're keeping her home now." He sighed and looked down at his cupped hands.

Simon nodded. "It must be hard for you. For her. Think about what I'm offering. We could make things easier for you, for your daughter. And you wouldn't want word of this to get out, would you?"

Hall looked up suddenly, his gaze intense, his voice lifting. "You still don't get it, do you? You just haven't got a clue. She's not the one with the problem, Leary. It's us. It's the boy."

"I don't—"

"I'm their father. The least I can do is to give them both the same chance. You see that, Leary? It's going to be easy for her. She's going to be one of *your* lot. She's going to have everything. They're both my kids, both of them. They deserve the same. They deserve everything I can give them."

Simon sat back as Hall's conviction washed over him and he slowly realised what the man was saying. There was too much to think about. He stood carefully, Hall's words ringing in his head: *She's not the one with the problem.*

He looked down at Hall—the big man staring blankly at the patch of carpet in front of him — and for the first time he saw more than just an Eater. This was a father concerned about his family, his children. And if the man could have a Photo kid... Simon stood there for a long time.

"I'll see what I can do," he said quietly, staring across at the man, no longer really seeing him. He turned and headed for the door.

Out on the porch, he stared up at the sky, looking

at the stars and thinking about what he was going to do.

-The End-

The Hero

The morning mist hung above the field where yesterday they'd seen death. The blackbirds were at work already picking at the unfortunates they had left behind. Tarben felt sick for them. There had been no chance to retrieve their fallen companions. He knew it had not been right, but there was little he could do. Verlak had talked to them long into the chill night, but now, in the cool vapor light of morning, Tarben felt less sure. For all he knew, Verlak had drawn them here to face their death as well. He had told them what to do, and then left them with assurances and little else and taken that damned greatsword with him.

"I tell you, Tarben, he's not going to come," Aryk muttered in his ear. "What we going to do then, eh?"

"We'll do what we have to do. Just be still."

"I don't mind telling you, I'm not feelin' right about this."

"Be still!" he hissed back. He could feel the sweat upon his palms despite the chill of the air.

The minutes wore on. They felt like hours. Aryk was fidgeting beside him, and Tarben wanted to move too, but he knew what Verlak had told them. They had to wait, here in this position, amongst their own dead, open and vulnerable and exposed. He flexed his fingers against his sword hilt, tension building inside him.

As the first rays of sunlight lanced across the open spaces from behind the hill, he heard movement. Phylux's troops were coming. Tarben could still not believe that he was standing there waiting, he and Aryk alone. The sounds of marching men and horses grew louder. The clank of metal and mutter of voices became more distinct.

Spearmen marched around the edge of the hill. The red of their shields glowed gold with the light of the morning sun. Horses flanked them on either side matching the pace of the footmen. Tarben could see more than the approaching force. In them, he saw his own death. Still, he gritted his teeth and waited.

"Hold, Aryk, hold," he whispered.

Finally, one of the riders spotted them and pointed. The warmth of the sun was dispersing the trailing fog and Tarben felt naked and alone.

The one obviously in charge gestured to his men to stop. He scanned the flat ground between them and the edge of the trees, looking for more of Tarben's men. He leaned across to one of his riders to say something. Although the sounds carried across the space between them, Tarben could not make out the words. The officer straightened in his saddle and laughed. Tarben gripped his sword hilt more tightly and stilled his urge to run. Aryk stood firm beside him looking nervously toward the spearmen arrayed across the field.

The officer leaned down and grabbed a spear from one of the soldiers standing beside him. Tarben felt his guts go cold as the rider hefted the spear in one hand and spurred his horse toward them. He reined in halfway across the intervening space. His horse pawed at the ground and its breath steamed as it snorted.

"Are you so eager to die?" he called across to them. Tarben merely stood and waited. The officer pointed up the hill with his spear, and Tarben followed its line. He had not noticed the priests appear, but they were there now. "Let them send you on your way. You clearly wish to join your companions." The officer narrowed his eyes. "But wait. You're the one they call Tarben. You, I would have alive."

The officer signaled to the horsemen behind him. Tarben could only stand and watch as they rode up to join their leader.

"Take this one," said the officer. "I will enjoy asking him some questions. Kill the other one. He's of no use to us."

Tarben swallowed back his nervousness, watching and waiting. He couldn't help thinking how they had come to be here.

oOo

It was the night before. Both of them sat in the small forest clearing, their horses tethered nearby. His men also clustered around, or stood further back through the trees, keeping watch.

"It always amazes me how you can eat after that."

"It always amazes me how you cannot," mumbled Aryk around a mouthful of dripping meat. He grinned and waved the chunk skewered on his knifepoint in Tarben's direction, the grease shining on his chin in the firelight. "I always get powerful hungry after a good scrap."

Aryk, the little cutpurse, had proved useful from time to time, but sometimes his hot temper and variable morals led Tarben to question. Still, Aryk had stood by him, unswerving in his loyalty. Tarben had to give him that much. From time to time, he wondered what Phylux had ever done to the thief, but his companion had always refused to be drawn.

"Aye, no doubt it's all the strength you lose running from the enemy."

Tarben ducked the lump of meat that sailed past his head.

"Now there. Look what you've done. Making me waste good food like that."

Tarben snorted and returned to staring at the fire. There were good fights and there were bad fights. Today had not been one of the good ones. It hadn't helped that Phylux had arrayed those cursed priests on the hill above them. Having a handful of snakes waved at you whilst being screamed at with the voices of damnation was enough to put anyone's mind off the battle. They'd lost some good men today. By the gods, he detested snakes. He listened to the sounds of the remaining few of his men filtering through the trees around him. When they'd started the day, there's been near to fifty. Farmers, blacksmiths, carpenters -- what sort of fighting force was that? Overall, they'd lost near two dozen of their fifty today. Fifty against two hundred didn't make for good odds, but these men had been fighting for their homes and land. They knew the area too, which should have swung things a little in their favour if fortune had chosen to smile at them, but it hadn't.

Tarben hunkered down to rest his forehead upon the cool hilt of his sword. He stared beyond it to the flickering embers and the hot ash of the fire. There had to be a way to get through and past those ranks of spearmen. He couldn't close with them; they were too tightly packed. If he tried to go around them, the ranks inclined and formed up to block him again. He cursed Phylux for his thoroughness; the man had trained his troops too well. Tarben had to admire him for the snakes too. That had been a good move. He wished he'd thought of it.

"Come on Tarben, eat something. You've got to keep your strength up." Aryk waved a freshly carved slab of meat at him, but Tarben gestured him away distractedly. There was thinking to do.

As if the spearmen were not bad enough, he had to contend with cavalry as well. The spear were slow, so there might have been a chance to get around them, but every time they had tried, those cursed skirmishers had cut off the approach. No, the horsemen protected the flanks too well. What he needed was something to punch through the center. If they broke the spear, then that was the backbone of Phylux's forces gone. The troops wouldn't have a chance of standing up to Tarben's men if that happened. The real trouble was that his men were too few. Yet another village had fallen under the heel of Lord Phylux. Since the death of his own village, Caerinford, Tarben had sworn to stop the petty lord. A year ago, less, who had heard of Phylux? But after the border wars and the drain of men from Vistara, the lordling had seen his opportunity, starting small and then little by little expanding his power and influence. Phylux cared nothing for the people or what he wrought, merely for power. It mattered not what he destroyed.

A quick breeze wafted smoke from their fire around their campsite. Tarben rubbed his eyes and grimaced. The smell of meat juices dripping from the spit sputtering in the coals gave it an acrid tang. His eyes stung, but it was more than just the smoke.

He had had a home once, long gone these many months. His mother, his sister taken, the farm put to the torch, the grain stores looted, and his father stretched out across the gateposts, lashed there and sightless from where the birds had done their work. Since that day, since his return from the army and the border wars, Tarben had wandered, gathering others around him to fight, to retain that which was theirs. Thoughts of simple revenge had long since passed.

oOo

Tarben woke to the feel of Aryk shaking his shoulder.

"Hey, Tarben, wake up. Somebody coming," Aryk hissed.

"What is it?" Tarben asked in a whisper.

"Don't know. Someone coming through the trees. Sounds like only one. Over behind us—out of the forest. What do you want to do?"

Tarben had already reached for his sword. His mind raced. It couldn't be anyone sent by Phylux. He wouldn't be that stupid. If it was someone alone, then they were probably only heading this way by accident.

"Are the rest awake?" Aryk nodded. "Tell them to hold then. Let me deal with this." Tarben got quietly to his feet.

"Tarben, what're you going to—?" Tarben stilled Aryk's whispered query with a gesture of his hand and Aryk scuttled off through the trees to convey the message.

Whoever it was plainly wasn't trying to sneak up on them. The footsteps were clearly audible, crunching through the leaves of the forest floor. Tarben relaxed and straightened from his crouch. He let the point of his weapon drop to the ground and casually leaned his weight on it while he waited. The noises of approach grew steadily closer. A hulking fur-clad figure emerged from between the trees and wandered into the dim glow of the fading fire. The stranger pulled up short and turned his thick-maned head from side to side as if suddenly confused by the light.

"Ho there, friend," Tarben called to him. "Can I be of some assistance?"

The stranger narrowed his eyes and peered at Tarben from beneath heavy brows. His scrutiny was unhurried as he scanned the rude campsite, Tarben's sword, and lingered for a moment on the remainder of Aryk's meal. The huge man grunted and tossed a heavy and travel-stained pack to the ground at his side. He reached slowly up behind his back and, just as slowly, revealed the metal of a large blade from behind the wild mass of his grey-streaked and matted hair. Tarben tensed. He grasped the hilt of his own weapon and dropped into a defensive crouch. The big man's face broke into a wide grin beneath his orange beard, and he threw back his head and bellowed a laugh.

"I don't want to fight you, little man. You look like you've had enough of fighting for one day as it is." He tossed his large blade to one side to fall on the ground near his pack. "And you can tell your friend over there to come out from behind that tree. He wouldn't get near me with that knife of his anyway. There's too much of me to stick." He slapped his broad belly and grinned.

Aryk slipped his dagger back into his belt as he stepped sheepishly from his place of concealment.

"Who are you?" Tarben asked, waving the point of his sword in the stranger's direction.

"Aye, who am I indeed?" The big man planted meaty hands upon his broad hips and grinned at them again. "What say you put down your sword? I'll come in and share a bit of warmth from your fire, carve myself a lump of that meat over there, and I can tell you all about who I am. Meantime, you can tell me all about who you are, and what you'd be doing in *my* forest."

Tarben had a moment's hesitation, and then glanced at Aryk, who shrugged in response. Slowly he lowered his sword.

"Fairly put," said Tarben. "Who are we to deny you hospitality? Come sit with us."

"Well, my thanks to you, friend. I would be grateful if your other companions would extend their hospitality too," the big man said as he inclined his head in the direction of the trees. Tarben nodded and raised his hand, telling his men to stand down. The stranger gave a satisfied nod and strode across the clearing to stand looking down at Tarben. He had left his greatsword where it lay, not even offering it a glance as he left it.

"So, little man ... they called me Verlak once. You may as well use the name. What shall I call you? You and your friend with the knife who would stick me now if he could." He looked at Aryk and gave a none-too-friendly grin. Aryk looked around nervously and carefully moved his hand back away from his knife hilt.

"I am Tarben, and this is Aryk."

"Good, now we have names, for what good they are. Will you sit with me, Tarben?" Verlak moved over to the fire and helped himself to a slab of cooling meat before settling his vast bulk on a stump by the fireside. Tarben crouched and watched across the embers as the giant of a man tore chunks from the meat and chewed noisily. When he had finished enough to have satisfied three men, the stranger smacked his lips, belched, and wiped his mouth with the back of one hairy paw.

"So, Verlak, tell me what brings you here."

"I should be asking that very same question, Tarben, not you."

Verlak peered at him across the flames that rose once again as Aryk stoked the embers. Aryk looked up from the patterns he was drawing in the dirt with his finger.

"You see, it is you who are here, in *my* home." Verlak made an expansive gesture at the forest around them. "It is you and your companions who are the guests at my hearth. Be sure not to abuse the privilege."

"Tarben, you going to let him talk like that?" Aryk said, a sneer on his face.

Verlak swung his head deliberately toward Aryk and fixed him with a look like thunder.

"You, little man, should hold your peace. I could tear your head from your body if I chose to."

Aryk jumped to his feet and scrabbled for his knife, but Tarben stilled him with an out-thrust hand.

Verlak grunted. "Aye, heed your friend, Aryk. He knows better than you. That is the reason you follow him, and not the other way about."

Tarben ignored the comment and continued his questioning. "What do you mean, *your* forest, Verlak? We see no marks or signs of ownership."

"Nor will you, Tarben. Nor will you. Ah, but it's mine all the same. I tolerate your presence here because it suits me. I tolerate it more than I do that pestilence that now sits beyond the trees." Verlak's apparent arrogance was beginning to annoy, but Tarben stilled his urge to do something about it. "I watched you and your men today, Tarben," the big man continued. It was not a good day for you. You lost more than you should have, but I think you know that."

"Aye, more than I should have." Tarben sighed. "But what is that to you?"

"You pit yourself against that scum Phylux," growled the big man. "That is reason for me to be interested. I would see aid given to any who stand in the way of Phylux's ambitions. He brings a darkness upon all of us. I watched you today, from up there upon the hill. You lost today, so tonight I am here." He looked across the fire and narrowed his eyes.

Aryk cleared his throat and spat into the flames. "Listen old man, we've heard what you've said, but we don't need no telling about what happened today. You've shared our fire; you've eaten our food. Time's right for you to be making your way to wherever you're going."

Verlak ignored him and continued speaking.

"What did you have on your mind trying to fight against spear and cavalry together, Tarben? The men you had, and those that you still have, they're no more than light skirmishers. The sort of numbers you'd need to face a force like that—"

"Why?" asked Tarben. "We hit them quickly, out of the trees. They shouldn't have been prepared for our strike. Surprise makes up for numbers. Anyway, why should I listen to you?"

"Because Tarben, I know a lot more about it than you might think. Don't let the appearance of an old man deceive you. Would you believe me more if I'd wandered in here in full armor? I think it probable, but then I doubt I would have had the hearing you've given me thus far. Besides, it's not very practical to wander about in full battle array." Verlak grinned through his beard and slapped his thighs. "I have reason for wanting to see you succeed. Phylux has ruled unopposed for too long. I should have done something about him when I had the chance. All you saw today was a raiding party. His forces are growing, and his position is strengthened with each new village or town he grinds beneath his heels. I've sat for too long, buried deep within these woods. Now I mean to act. I can help you Tarben, and so too, you can help me."

Aryk snorted. "You talk pretty words for an old hermit living in the middle of a forest."

"And if you know what's for the good, you'll listen to what I have to offer, little man."

"Aryk has a point, Verlak. Why should we listen to you?" said Tarben.

"Will you not take me on faith then?"

Tarben merely stared across at him.

Verlak continued with a sigh. "No, I should not have expected it. Aye, well, if I must, I must."

Verlak wiped the palms of his large hands on the

fur of his coat. He leaned forward and stretched out his arms in front of him. He hunched his shoulder and moved one hand above the other, fingers curled as if they held something more than empty air. Aryk glanced between Tarben and Verlak. Tarben could see his companion was tensed, ready to leap in attack, and he could see the concentration etched across Verlak's brow. The old man would be a fool if he were to try something now. Tarben watched and waited. Verlak narrowed his eyes and stared at the space above his curling fingers.

He gave a mighty roar and stood. A loud noise split the air above the old man's hands. Suddenly, those hands were empty no longer. Between them, he held the hilt of a massive sword. Orange sparks flickered up and down its length.

Tarben's diminutive companion fell back in shock and his jaw dropped open. Tarben's own eyes widened in disbelief. He could not possibly have seen what had just happened. Perhaps the old man had bewitched them somehow. He glanced back over his shoulder to where Verlak had dropped his sword, but the leaf-littered ground beside the discarded pack was empty. Slowly, he turned back to face Verlak. He chased for thoughts, but there were none.

Verlak allowed the weight of his blade to fall back against his shoulder. He looked beyond Tarben to the trees surrounding their clearing, then back to Tarben. His face broke into a humorless smile.

"So, will you listen to me now, Tarben? At least I think I have your attention." He chuckled wryly. "If you would grant me the favor of telling your companions back there to join us, or at least put up their weapons, then we can talk more. They have seen enough blood spilled today; would you not say?"

Tarben shook himself and motioned vaguely toward the surrounding undergrowth. He didn't even bother to look as his group of battle-weary men moved one by one into the clearing. They would only act on his signal. His attention was on Verlak.

"Let me tell you something more of myself, Tarben. I've been around for a long time. I *know* Phylux, and he knows me. My name is Verlak. Some have called me Verlak the Bear." Tarben heard a sharp intake of breath behind him. "Ah, I see the name is known. You may be too young to have heard it, but there are some who will not be."

Tarben rubbed his forehead. He *had* heard the name somewhere before, but it was a long, long time ago. He was still reeling from the shock of what he had just witnessed, and, though he groped for words, none came. He glanced across at Aryk, who barely managing to salvage some of the little dignity he possessed, maneuvered himself back into a sitting position. His small companion brushed twigs and leaves from his hands but forgot to close his mouth.

"Tarben, I've seen what you've done here," Verlak continued. "I will sing your praises for that. Whipping this band of outlaws and villagers into some sort of discipline takes natural skill. But I fear it's not enough. You can lead men, Tarben, and that is a skill worth having, but more is needed if you would prevail."

"What do you mean?" Tarben asked him. "Oh, you may as well sit, and put up your sword. I think you have our attention now, and I have the feeling that the night will be a long one."

Verlak smiled across the fire at him and nodded his great head once, before doing just that. As he laid the broad blade on the ground beside him, Tarben marked the green gem set at the pommel. He had heard tales of a sword such as this, one that conjured fire and directed its strike. It had a name.

Aryk had crept up beside him. "Is that…?" he whispered in Tarben's ear.

Tarben shook his head to still him.

"Good, then let us begin," said the old man. He had noted their nervous glances in the direction of the now resting blade and the corners of his eyes wrinkled in amusement. His hand reached out to gently caress the hilt of the giant sword lying on the ground beside him. "I see you may have some knowledge of my old friend Soulstealer here but pay her no mind. We must begin."

"What does he mean, Tarben? Begin what?" Aryk said looking confused. He scratched the back of his head and screwed up his face. "Far as I see it, we don't need no advice from some old man comes wandering out of the forest. We don't know nothing about him. What I see is, we're doing all right on our own. Sure, he's got a fancy sword, but that don't mean nothing to me. What we need's a hero, not advice from some hermit thinks he knows this and that. If that sword of yours is so good old man, then maybe you want to play at being a hero for us, but that's about it."

"Listen, little man." Verlak narrowed his eyes and swung his large frame to face him. "Talk of heroes is what gets you dead. Heroes don't just happen. Put all your faith in one man, in a particular magic or a special weapon and you'll wind up deader than those you left behind today. I could come and fight with you. What good would that do? Phylux would concentrate his attention here, pour troops in from surrounding areas as soon as he heard. As I said, Phylux knows me. You have neither numbers nor experience. My presence would do you more harm than good. What you need is a strategy and a plan. You can't win a battle on faith alone. Nobody's a hero if they're dead, and there's nobody that can't be replaced. A fighting force is like an animal. It has parts of it that do different jobs, but it functions as a whole thing. Bits and pieces of it don't go wandering off. If they did, then the creature falls apart. Yes, I have a blade, a powerful blade, but you need more than that."

"So, what's that got to do with us?" asked Aryk skeptically.

"That's what was happening today. I watched your attack. Small numbers of your group ran in and tried to break through. There were too many of them for you and they were too well placed. They worked as a unit, whereas you did not. The cavalry guarded the flanks of the spearmen, and the spearmen did their job by keeping you channeled to where the horsemen could hit you and cause the most damage. After each skirmish, they could retreat behind the spears and regroup, safe and protected when they were most vulnerable."

Aryk chewed his finger as he thought about what the old man was telling them.

Verlak continued. "What good would a hero have done you today, little man? What would an old man with a special sword have done for you?"

There was a long silence.

"What would you suggest we do, Verlak?" Tarben asked after the pause. "What choice did we have?"

"I'm not sure, Tarben, but I think your little friend may have given me an idea."

oOo

Tarben dropped into a crouch, waving his sword in front of him. He could feel Aryk behind him pressed up against his back as they circled as one, ready to slash at the first horseman who approached. The riders started to circle too, wary of the sharp blades being waved toward them. Tarben glanced through the ring of riders, over toward the spearmen, who now stood relaxed, watching the scene before them. The time had come. He took a deep breath, planted his feet, and stood straight.

"You," he spoke to the horsemen that surrounded him. "It's time you left this place." He passed the hilt of his sword from one hand to the other, and drove the blade, point first into the ground in front of him. The rider directly in front of him grinned.

A mighty bellow echoed across the valley from the hill above them. There, silhouetted in the sunlight, a huge fur-clad figure grabbed one of the priests, lifted him high in the air, and tossed him down the face of the hill. The other priest was already running. The officer's eyes grew wide with shock as the white-robed body tumbled down the hillside.

"Now, my companions," Tarben called in as loud a voice as he could muster. "Your time has come." He picked up his sword and swept the blade in a wide arc. "Come! Come back from the dead and join the living."

From all around, came the stirrings of motion. What had seemed to be corpses now started climbing to their feet, weapons in hand. Rapidly, they advanced upon the horsemen with moans and cries.

The officer was the first to be dragged from his horse and stilled with a blade across his throat. The other riders spun their horses in confusion. Tarben jumped at the nearest and dragged him to the ground. His blade made short work of the downed man. One by one, his men attacked the exposed horsemen and one by one, the horsemen died.

Within minutes there was nothing left of the cavalrymen except their riderless mounts. Verlak had been right. Separate the parts and the animal will die. Tarben smiled as he turned toward the spearmen who now milled in confusion. He broke into a trot toward them. A glance up at the hillside showed Verlak, now with greatsword held high above his head, charging down toward the foot soldiers as well, orange fire coursing up and down the blade. Not a single one of his men had reached the spearmen when they broke and ran as one. Two or three would get away, but his lighter-clad fighters easily overtook the rest. Tarben gave up the chase and stood surveying the results.

The old warrior had told him something during the night; something that stood out more than all the other words that had passed between them. You don't become a hero by losing a fight.

Verlak wandered across the field toward Tarben, picking his way among the fallen, and the groups of Tarben's men who now stood congratulating each other on the empty field, still dressed as the dead they had left behind on the previous day. As the old warrior approached, Tarben could see his grin.

Verlak reached out with one large hand and gripped his shoulder. "Today, Tarben," he said. "Today *you* start to become the hero you seek, not me. This day is just the first. May you become the legend that we need, and not the sword."

Tarben scanned the bodies littering the field and knew Verlak was right.

The old man grunted, shouldered his ancient blade, and lumbered off towards the trees.

Tarben was left standing there, watching the broad retreating back. He thought of calling after him, something, but now…now there was tomorrow to think about.

-The End-

The Secret Properties of Glass

Peter was a pastime. Somewhat reluctantly, he knew that was a true answer, though dwelling on it did him little good. How you could be a pastime to yourself was sometimes just beyond him sometimes.

He rubbed his brow, then returned with a sigh to the half-warm mug of coffee steaming vaguely in the chill morning air. And so, he thought, the ritual had begun. Chin on hand, elbow on table, he stared out the window through his own reflected image, considering. There he was, superimposed on all that was his -- all of it, and yet none. And there lay the rub.

A sudden pain dragged him back to the immediate with the realisation that he'd been biting his little finger as he sat. He regarded the purple and white indentations and then looked out onto the roadway with set jaw. It was their fault. It always would be. Reality was vindictive. Reality had teeth, but it hid them in his own mouth. He shook his head and sighed.

Drink the coffee. Swallow and swallow again.

He swirled the silt in the bottom of his mug for one last mouthful and the radio said nothing. Even had it, it would have been beyond his attention. It chattered at him every morning with the rest of the world. It was breakfast.

He switched it off and breakfast was finished.

Upturning his mug on the sink, he took the time to narrow his eyes at a cockroach. They didn't bother him, but the gesture was good. Cockroaches were real. He knew that. They were inside those private places that no other could see. He knew because of the way they scuttled into darkened corners when they spied him, or scattered hither and thither when he switched on a light in their private rooms at night. They knew Peter was real too and this bothered their insect minds. He achieved a certain satisfaction from the occasional cockroach. Sometimes he wondered whether they might not trade places the cockroaches and him. Let him scuttle away to secluded corners. Let them face the siege.

But enough; it was time to find his spectacles. Strange how an extra layer of glass might help him to see more clearly. Although he wondered about that, it further confirmed his suspicions.

Layers within layers.

Peter Wilmott. Mister Wilmott. Yes, what can I do for you? A tone of suspicion in the voice. No one called him Peter. Gray suit, white shirt, grey tie, white socks, black and polished shoes -- Mister Wilmott had arisen for one more day with both 't's intact. The uniform was uniform. Peter stood for a moment surveying Mister Wilmott and nodded with satisfaction.

He would walk to work, as usual. He didn't own an automobile, or at least not now. He had once, but it had become a liability. Old and battered, it had held together until he started to fix it, and then it fell apart, seemingly as a punishment for his actions. He decided that it was better to watch the world through murky windows or wedged between crowded bodies rather than drive.

Glass within glass.

Sometimes, just sometimes, he would wonder about the properties of glass, as if there were some hidden meaning to the substance. What was there?

Something he could learn? Something to fight the fangs of the day? No ... it was more likely another illusion in which his attention could founder.

Looking around, he located the sombre black case he habitually carried, more as a ritual than necessity. He gripped it firmly on his daily march, held at arm's length by his side as if it were a bomb, primed to explode. Black, anonymous, innocuous yet deadly with its hidden warning, it helped his walk to work, giving silent protection. Reaching a hand down to shuffle about inside, he checked that everything was there, knowing quite well that it would be. Not that it would have made a scrap of difference if any of the accumulated papers were missing. They looked efficient when he opened the case to the world. If someone sat close in a café, he could pull out the case and retreat with ease. Satisfied that everything was in order, he headed out, locking the door behind him.

As usual, Peter watched the world as Mister Wilmott walked. The case bumped against his leg, forming an even rhythm. He confined his careful stride to the pavement's outer edge, so he could easily avoid the eyes of those passing in the other direction. He focused on small casually dropped pieces of paper, or scraps blown into the gutter, their lettering starting to fade. Thus occupied, his eyes down, he was unreachable. True, he had dual protection, and he was quite amused by the way others were reluctant to engage the eyes of one wearing spectacles. They were an indication of weakness, a disability. After all, people should only associate with their equals. Very occasionally, he would be daring and shoot a sidelong glance at a passer-by to see their quick avoidance. Were they aware that he was testing their solidity, or was there some other reason for their reluctance? He had his suspicions there too.

One day, a day such as this, Peter had been pleasantly surprised by the appearance of a dead cat in the gutter near his house. A car had probably hit it, but there seemed to be no visible marks of injury. Peter wondered if it had not been a sign itself, the way it grinned sightlessly at him as he strode past. He quickly achieved a sense of fellowship with its knowing smile, fangs bared at the world and grinning, grinning and he began to look forward to their daily meetings. During those few days, the cat became quite an intimate acquaintance. Sadly, it wasn't long before some faceless city worker carted the unsightly corpse from public view. It had saddened him to see it gone, but that was the way things worked outside. He sometimes wished he'd thought to pause, to crouch down in front of it and engage it in conversation. Would it have answered back? Would it have told him of the things that mattered?

Peter arrived at his building and headed for the stairs. Faded green and white linoleum tiles and the smell of polish were far safer than the hazards of the elevator. The first floor with its creamy gloss paint and frosted glass windows passed him by. This was his morning discipline. Some people exercised; he showed courage. Mondays were a little perilous, for he'd had the entire weekend to relax with himself. In a way, it was good that he was a trifle early, for it gave him time to prepare. He entered, and took up position behind his desk. It was a good desk, high, solid, and firm. He ran his fingers over the top, feeling the grain. There were patterns there. Sometimes, when he was wandering in his thoughts, he would attempt to decipher them, but never with much success.

Adjusting his chair, he sank back into the imitation leather and, resting his elbows upon the thick arms, he steepled his fingers in front of his face. He reached up to adjust the tilt of his spectacles and tried again. He judged the position in his mind's eye and felt it was right. He reached across, turned the page of the desk calendar, and leaned forward to read the proverb for the day. It was the usual garbage to be found on those things -- words spoken by legendary men to guide the less legendary. They meant nothing, but he thought it good to read them all the same.

Peter was ready now, so he sat staring at nothing, waiting. Stare out the window, Mister Wilmott. Look as if you're making plans for the day. He could barely be doing anything else; the dusty pane looked out on a bare brick wall. The grime-streaked window reminded him -- though he had an important office, it did not warrant an important view. He wondered why that was. He deserved better, because underneath the careful exterior of Mister Wilmott sat Peter.

And Peter was clever by design.

Knowledge was what it was all about. It was like names. The secret power that one could have over another. He had decided some time ago, that when he had the clues to the world's secret names, he would know it and thereby gain the power to control it. So, he had sat back and observed. He watched cars and he watched pedestrians. He spent hours contemplating the growth of grass or the shape of clouds. Mister Wilmott could walk about the face of the earth alone and untouched. To travel and see, yet not be seen. This was his goal.

It had been quite simple to prepare. He purchased the right clothes; he had seen them in a magazine. He adopted the right stance, and even braved a barber with regularity -- one of those silent methodical types that worked away and left him alone. A brief talk of the weather or the latest sports results was as far as it went, though actually Peter knew nothing about sports.

Later he purchased a television.

The television excited him for a while, with its talk of real-life drama. He would sit, straining, transfixed by every word and action. Then he began to see. It was even less substantial than the rest. He finally switched it off for good and it sat there in the corner, mute. He used it to stand a vase on. Now and then, he would fill the vase with flowers.

After a time, he began to frequent coffee lounges. The devotion slowly transferred itself to the coffee, and he sought places where the coffee was best. It mattered not that the waitresses talked about him in low tones and snickered behind raised hands, for he walked, he sat, and he learned. But still there was something absent, and the absence, the lack, made him strangely afraid. He was not ashamed of his fear, but he had to act as its sentinel.

And so had come Mister Wilmott.

Just then, the phone tried very hard to ring, pulling him from his musings. Peter sensed it in the back of his neck. The bland little receptionist who sat meticulously filing and polishing her nails had not yet arrived. Only the small soft-plastic doll with the bright orange hair marked her place, like a bookmark. This was where she was supposed to be when she came back. Today, however, Peter was early. Downstairs, somewhere, an answering machine dutifully played its message.

A few moments later, and there were the faint stirrings of life below. He reached down to the lower drawer, and drew out a sheaf of copied pages. Dutifully he bowed his head over them, placing a hand on his forehead. Just the right position. Here was Mister Wilmott hard at work. Yes, you could disturb him, but only at a distance. Peter glanced at his watch while he read. With her usual unerring punctuality, his secretary would make her appearance on the stroke of nine. He heard the bustle of arrival outside his door. He listened as she placed her bag down, re-arranged the work of the cleaners at her desk. He heard the pause as she made the final adjustments to her face. He waited for the inevitable. There it was -- the sound of her hand upon his door. The slight creak as the handle turned. The vague pressure as the air moved within the room. The door swung inward, and she poked her head around the corner, abruptly.

"Good morning, Mister Wilmott." She ducked back out of sight before he could really see her face.

"Humph," he grunted at the retreating head.

Fifty-five, competent and organized to the point of nausea. Peter was sure she had an answer to every problem. If he had been a monarch, she would have been the peroxide power behind the throne. Still, he and Mister Wilmott had different tastes, and she was the proper secretary for a man of his position. She kept the world from his door.

And she was back.

"These articles require your attention, Mister Wilmott. They must go in the afternoon mail. Mister Peckham has an appointment to see you at eleven, and the staff is collecting for a farewell gift for Mister Oliver. I've taken the liberty of putting you down for ten. Now, is there anything I can get you? A cup of coffee perhaps?"

Mister Wilmott nodded, and she withdrew. Yes, coffee would be good. It would be just how Mister Wilmott liked it. Peter hated that. How did she always get it right?

Peter waited, knowing she would come and go, and barring the minor interruptions -- papers that needed signing, decisions to be made -- leave him to the rest of his day. And now, that day was brooding behind him, and though he tried to shrug it off, the feeling stayed. The world was growling at him silently, and if he listened hard enough, he could almost make out the syllables of its voice. He glanced back over his shoulder, but for the moment, the day didn't seem to be there.

Without fuss, his secretary returned with the promised coffee and retired. It did little to aid the unease nestled deep in his stomach. When the appropriate amount of time had elapsed, she reappeared, taking the empty cup with her. How did she know when he was done?

The phone rang then.

"Call for you, Mister Wilmott. Shall I put it through?"

"Did they give a name?"

"No, sir."

Peter thought for a moment. He wasn't expecting a call.

"Oh well. I'm rather busy, but you may as well put them through." Mister Wilmott sighed and Peter tensed, listening.

"Is this Mister Wilmott?" asked the faint voice on the other end. Static crackled across the line.

"Yes, speaking."

"Mister Peter Wilmott?"

"Yes, that's right," replied Peter, faintly disturbed by the use of his first name.

"Well, Peter, we need to talk."

"Who is this?" Peter asked, his voice unsteady.

Only white noise met his query.

He held the receiver away and stared at it. Nobody knew him by his first name. No one.

It couldn't have been a wrong number. They had asked for him by name, and why had they hung up? Perhaps the line had been cut off. Yes, that was it. They would ring back in a few minutes and finish what they were going to say. After all, there was no sense in irrational panic. That wasn't going to help anything.

He spent the rest of the day casting furtive glances at the phone. As he waited, he felt the huge dark shape mouthing silent words behind his back.

For the rest of the day, despite his willing it, the phone simply refused to ring again. He stared at it for a while, but that did no good either. When he finally heard the bustling of the various secretaries scraping themselves together to go to their respective nights, he dragged himself out of the report he was writing, and, carefully placing the top back on his pen, slid it into his jacket pocket. He patted it gently to make sure it was in place, just so. As she always did about this time, his secretary poked her head around the door.

"Time to leave, Mister Wilmott. I'll be going then. Good night."

He harrumphed his reply, and waited for her to retreat. After the clacking of her shoes had faded down the corridor, he scraped his papers into a neat pile. In a few moments, his case was primed, and he was ready to leave. Instead, he sat back and stared at the wall, but it told him nothing.

Then he looked at the desk.

He looked out the window at the bricks. It was already dark outside. That was good. He shoved the pile of papers away in their place and gave the office one last look before heading out, closing the door firmly behind him.

Dark was good.

Peter liked the colder seasons. It became dark earlier, and he could fold the shadows around him, hug the edge of the pavement and use the darkness as a shield. The glossy streets and the occasional flashes of illumination of a passing car did little to expose his presence. It was far more effective sticking to the sides at night, for the window lights didn't really reach that far. Not enough to matter.

There was a slight breeze, tasting of ice, yet slick with the grime of the city. Everything here was oiled, and the bends in the glass fronts distorted enough to be pleasant. He tilted his head to one side and looked for patterns in the lines of light.

He passed the taxi rank with its collection of

drivers standing huddled and blowing on their hands while they talked. They waited too, but it was different. Sometimes they glanced sideways from their conversations, as though they were dreading, rather than expecting a fare.

He hurried on past.

More display windows drifted by. Mannequins watched him with bored expressions as he eyed their hard plastic bodies. They stuck their noses in the air and turned away, watching some distant scene with synthetic eyes. He wondered what thoughts ran through their heads. What would they say to him if he could suddenly strike up a conversation? Did they have names he could address them by? With the position of their heads and faces, they thought too much of themselves anyway.

Not long later, he reached his destination. Bright red letters announced that tasty food was to be had inside. He negotiated the step and winced a little as he walked into the light. As he shuffled into the steam and noise, people glanced up from their plates inquisitively, then returned to pushing mouths full of greasy food between snatches of conversation.

Peter walked over to one of the darker tables near a wall, and pulled out a chair facing the door. Carefully he placed his case down beside the table, and settled himself to wait. His elbows resting on the plastic surface, his hands steepled in front of his mouth, his eyes a little narrowed and peering over the top of his spectacles, he waited and watched. The lives waltzed around him. He was a wallflower. He was a cuckoo nesting in their home, and he went unnoticed all the same.

"Can I help you?" said a bored female voice over

his head.

"What? Oh, yes ... ah, could you bring me ... a coffee? Yes, a coffee ... and, ah ... I will have lasagne please. Yes, that will do."

"That'll be eight fifty, please," she said automatically, hand outstretched.

Mister Wilmott paid her, and she left. Peter liked the atmosphere. Payment up front, the transaction completed with the minimum of fuss, no ceremony.

Every time he was here, a large ceiling fan always attracted his attention. Glossy metal swinging around, urging his hand to caress the softness of its curve. He watched the fan for a short time, then felt his eyes drawn down and away. Someone was watching him -- watching Mister Wilmott. Peter looked across to where the other sat, pretending to be casting his gaze elsewhere.

The watcher was hunched over his table. He hid large bright eyes with his hand, but Peter had seen their alertness. Pasty flesh and a long broad, almost pointed nose extending beneath fine brows in a wide round face. His wispy hair floated about his pate, stirred by the motion of the fan.

Peter watched.

The little man toyed with the food in front of him. Now and again, he would glance up, and simultaneously, both he and Peter would look the other way. But before that scurrying glance, there would be that moment of *contact*. Peter swallowed. Did this have something to do with the call? A cold, uneasy feeling developed in the pit of his stomach. Peter was certain, now. He was being scrutinised. It was as if the man was sizing him up, ready to pounce. And now that he thought about it, the man's features looked almost feline. But who would want to study *him*?

In those few moments, he cultivated his outrage. Forcing his anger into courage, he dropped his gaze and met the other man's, keeping his eyes fiercely open, not even risking a blink. The man lowered his hand from his brow, and just as fiercely stared back.

Impasse.

Then, his opponent screwed up his napkin and threw it on the plate before him. There was a hidden violence in the act, as if he had just thrown down a paper gauntlet. With just the hint of a smile quirked across his lips, the man rose. Peter was horrified. He was going to come across.

The man gave one firm, deliberate wink, and turning on his heel, strode out the door and into the night.

Peter stared after him.

Everything was fine. He was imagining things. It was fine. He chewed on his finger, his attention drifting back up to the fan.

About five minutes later, a plate of greasy lasagne slapped itself down on the table in front of him, shortly followed by a cup and a saucer swimming with spilled coffee. He narrowed his eyes at the retreating waitress.

The food was up to its usual lack of form and appeal, but the coffee was strong. He really only came here for the coffee. It was bitter and hot. He could bury himself in such a cup and fade the rest of the world about him. Each swallow occupied his senses with a mild rapture. The searing bitterness gave him a clarity that was more than just the caffeine within.

After finishing the coffee, he ploughed through the waiting pasta. It was oily and only slightly warm. It would give him indigestion later, but he shovelled it down. The experience was worth it.

He watched his hands playing idly with the remnants on the plate in front of him. The leavings left slick little orange trails as he pushed them about the plate. A tiny ball of meat, a sliver of limp pasta. Back and forth, he watched the fork move, not really seeing its motion at all. When he looked up again, most of the other patrons had left. Fluorescent lights and smoky air crowded his head with haze.

He beckoned the waitress and ordered another coffee.

He grunted in satisfaction as it burned his tongue. The scald would remain for a time, dividing his attention, clarifying his focus. Pain, with its clean hard edges would do that. It would allow him to view things with just that little bit extra abstraction he needed. He drank it quickly. Then, satisfied that he was suitably distracted, he grabbed his case, trickled some change onto the table and strode firmly out the door.

The night had grown colder. His preoccupation with the thorns in his reality had dragged the minutes into hours.

Gathering his determination, he set out for home. Mister Wilmott adopted a stern face. Keep away from me. I'm not one to be trifled with. Eyes down, dutifully watching the passing gutter. Deep thought. Solving a problem.

As soon as Peter moved away from the bright lights, he felt better. He lifted his head and took in more of the surrounds. The streets he chose were ones infrequently travelled by wandering people and passing cars. Many trees lined the paths and blocked him from casual view. Each crack in the concrete he greeted with familiarity. Each verge of grass was used to his tread.

He detoured through the park on the way home. There was something about the space so devoid of people. He could expand and stretch without feeling that it would leave him naked. The smell of grass and trees was good in the darkness, for there were no lights in this park to force him to view.

For a while, he wandered.

The night clasped itself about him and he started to feel secure in the sound of his own footsteps firm against the solid ground. They echoed about and within him. They helped keep his mind occupied, like the scald that burned in his mouth. Something to think about.

Then ahead, just outside of the park, something caught his attention.

Peter stepped from beneath the shadowed trees to look. He crossed the pavement and stopped at the gutter's edge. Whatever it was, it lay hunched against the curb -- something gray and striped, with fur bunched in damp clumps. And it grinned.

Peter was sure that the cat had been taken away, that someone had removed it to leave him alone and floundering. Yet here it was. Was it even the same one?

Gently he placed his case down as he stooped to get a better view. It looked like the same one. Its sightless eyes stared along the length of the curb as if testing the angles. Peter adjusted the spectacles on his nose and peered closer. The lips were a little dry, and pulled back from the fangs. The grin was there, and it was the same grin. He rocked back on his heels, pulled the spectacles from his face, wiped them on his shirt and replaced them as he considered. Then he leaned forward again.

"Hello, old friend," he said.

"Hello, Peter," said the cat.

Relief washed down upon him like the taste of coffee. The cat knew his name; it had to be the one.

"It's Mister Wilmott," said Peter.

"But we both know it's Peter."

Peter hunched down and thought. Perhaps this was another device after all. He chewed at his finger and frowned.

"How are you?" he asked.

"I'm dead," said the cat.

Peter peered closer. The clumped fur showed the ribs beneath as if the cat was collapsing from the inside. He could see the even line of the backbone.

"Why do you grin like that?"

"Because it's amusing. Can't you see?"

Peter adjusted his spectacles and looked up and down the street. He looked back down at the cat. Was it trying to tell him something?

"No I can't," he said.

"But you can, Peter. I'm dead."

Peter frowned, and then came realization and his insides went cold. The presence was back behind him, mouthing. He felt his shoulders tense. What would he do if someone happened by and saw him here, hunched over the gutter, talking to a dead cat. Mister Wilmott would not be enough.

"I must go," he said.

"No, Peter, wait," said the cat. "I have things to show you, and then you'll understand. We couldn't talk earlier, but now we can."

An ant crawled out of the cat's mouth, traversed the drying lip, then walked across the sparse facial hair toward the eye socket. He wondered how long the cat had lain here waiting for him. He wondered why it hadn't told him these things before.

Peter checked up and down the street again. If he was careful, he might appear as if Mister Wilmott was a little the worse for wear, that he had too much to drink, or was feeling ill. He leaned over, supporting his weight on one hand. That way they would avoid him, steer a path away.

"Yes," he said quietly. "Tell me."

"Look into my eyes," said the cat as it grinned at him.

Peter stared into flat sightless hollows. On one side, there was something there, like a drum skin stretched taut. The other side was empty and hollow. Black crust rimed the edge. He felt for his case, making sure it was safe.

"That's it. Look into my eyes."

"I'm looking. But I don't know what I'm supposed to see."

"And that's the problem, Peter. Now concentrate."

He narrowed his focus, shutting out the world.

He was inside the cat's head, with the cat beside him. It was a vast dark place. It echoed around him. He felt for his spectacles, afraid that he had lost them, but they were there in his hand. He was worried about

Mister Wilmott.

"He'll be just fine," said the cat beside him. "See there?"

Peter looked where the cat was pointing. Large round orbits showed vague images beyond them. Nothing moved, just a long line stretched far and away. He could see the grain of the concrete stretching into the distance. Peter moved closer to the wide openings and peered up and off to the side. There crouched Mister Wilmott, staring back at him. Behind him stood trees and the park framed against the sky. The only shadow lurking there was that cast by the trees, and the one that stretched beside him in Mister Wilmott's shape.

"It doesn't matter where you hide yourself away," said the cat. "They can't get to you."

"But I don't understand what you're telling me. Of course they can't get to me. Everything's there to stop them. I've seen to that."

"But every one of them, every single one, is just like you. It doesn't matter if you're looking through spectacles or looking through the eyes of a cat, or through a window, or through a wall. It's the same. They all build their own personal fortresses to maintain the distance, and no matter what you do, you cannot breach those walls. No one can."

"I've seen them try. This is just another trick."

He stepped closer to the eyeholes, missing the protection of the case in his hand. Mister Wilmott crouched there staring down. Was the eye like a window? Was this like glass? Shielded and protected looking out upon the world. But the darkness behind him did not threaten. It just *was*. And the cat was his friend.

A friend removed and returned. The cat knew his secret name and yet it held no special power.

"What's so funny, cat?" he asked.

"The funny thing is that it's all so simple. What you took for conspiracy was construction. There are no secret names. There is no power. There is no hidden magic. The only magic is that which you make yourself. The only real magic is here inside my head. That's what's funny."

"But how am I to know that?"

"If you think hard you will see. The beast behind your back is one of your own making. When you saw that man tonight, you almost made contact -- almost. When you think about cockroaches, you know that you disturb them because you're real, and yet they don't disturb you. Why is that? They are as real as you or I. Look out there. What do you see?"

"I see nothing," said Peter. "I see the park and the trees. I see the night. I see Mister Wilmott."

"Yes. You see nothing. And without you, he's nothing, he's empty. Without us being here, there would be nothing here either."

"I'm still not sure I understand."

"I think you do, Peter," said the cat. "Now go home, back to your place of private walls, and think about that. And when you have doubts, think about the cockroaches. Trade places with them so that you can see just what *is* real."

Mister Wilmott stood. He picked up his case and with his other hand, he removed his spectacles. He stared at them, there in his hand and then slowly, he slipped them into his inside pocket. He looked down at the dead cat lying in the gutter, wiped his hand across his forehead, and stepped slowly out onto the street.

"Goodbye, old friend," he said.

The cat said nothing.

-The End-

Want

I lie here alone, and the memory of him calls to me in the still of night. Now nothing more than emptiness stretches between us. That voice, his voice, murmurs in my head and it stirs something deep inside, though I have never heard words from his lips. I give his voice shape and texture in my thoughts. I can almost feel those lips now, soft like the touch of fragile wings upon my skin, but still the ache will not leave me.

I was used to being alone. I didn't even give it much mind after the old woman had gone, not at first. But sometimes it would eat at me, and I would think somehow to change it. After I wished so hard, after the rituals in the dark of night – only then did things become different. It was only then that I happened upon the pool.

Many a time had the old woman warned me that art bore its own cost. I had paid her words little mind. I was young; I had little idea what that cost might be, but I know it now.

She showed me the rituals and the ingredients I needed. There in forest darkness had I muttered the words and wished. I tossed the powders into the flames, watching as sparks shot skywards through the leaves above. And those sparks carried with them my desire. I waited expectantly. When nothing happened, I put it from my mind. Only well after I came across the pool did I understand the true nature of the power I had summoned so casually.

I stumbled upon it, deep within the trees buried in the heart of my woodland garden. Forest light filtered in shafts through the branches and the scent of damp leaves filled my nostrils. It was collecting time – the time when I gathered small plants and herbs for the medicines I mixed for the afflicted. As seasons change, so do the plants that grow with them. Each season has its collecting time, and at such times, I wandered through the woods, gathering what I needed for the various preparations that were my livelihood.

I thought I knew those woods, knew every path and twist. Before the old woman passed, she had shown me the ways and where things grew and in what quantities. This one was good for this ailment, that one for another. Then, when she had passed from this life, all that knowledge became mine. The birds became my company, and the woodland creatures became the passers-by that broke my solitude. Not those who came to seek my remedies and charms. They did so hesitantly with downcast eyes. They would not have me in the village or even near it. But they came to me for their cures and salves all the same.

Once, there was a young man who came seeking a cure for his ailing mother. Perhaps bolder than the rest, he was fair of face, and he looked at me sidelong when he thought I could not see. For several weeks, he came to visit me, and for a time, I thought to make him mine, to feel his rough hands upon me, to draw him close. On one such day, when I handed him his package, all wrapped in leaves, I contrived to let my fingers linger, but he drew back from the touch as if burned, panic in his eyes. I knew then that it was not to be.

He, like others, never returned.

Some nights I thought of him, thought about how his bare tanned chest would feel pressed up against my naked breast, his hand held tight against the hollow of my back. I thought about his breath warm in my ear, coming hard and fast and of his sweet salt sweat mixing with mine in the firelight.

He must have spoken about what I had done and what he feared. It was weeks before another came, a farmer's wife, all red-faced and rough-handed and eager to be gone. Only women came then, or old men. It seemed they even feared to send the young village boys as they had so many times before. They left me with only the memory. And it was then, in my desperation, I sought out the old woman's instructions scratched in her spidery script in the book she had left behind. It took time for me to realize the connection with what I had done.

It was late afternoon, in the long summer days where evening stretched into night and the warm breezes stirred the air between the trees. There was a clearing where I knew I could find certain mushrooms I needed for my remedies. They grew only in late summer and then only when the rains had come. I had been wandering the paths, gathering here and there and the clearing was to be my last stop for the day. When I collected all I came for, I planned to rest there, listening to the sounds of the summer evening, my back against a tree, the scents, and noises of life all around me.

As I stepped along the path, ducking low beneath the branches, a sound came, an unfamiliar sound. I stopped to listen. The splash of water came from up ahead. I waited for it to come again, but only the rustle of leaves and bird song filtered through the trees.

Cautiously I made my way forwards, slipping around the sides of huge trunks and peering along the path, wary. How could the sound of water be coming from a place where no water should be?

Silently I slipped towards the clearing edge, and hugged my body close behind a massive trunk. Gently, so gently, I eased my face around, peering past the moss-covered bark. And despite myself, I gasped. There, where once had lain a clearing covered in grass and sprinkles of summer flowers, sat a pool. Or, at least, I thought it was a pool. It stretched almost the length of the clearing. For a while I was confused, but looking back, I know now that deep inside I knew the truth of it.

For several beats, there was nothing. I stayed still. So still. An arrow of ripples traversed the surface heading for the opposite side. Then, right at the arrow's tip, something broke the surface — a head and shoulders — long dark hair and berry-brown skin.

I ducked back behind the trunk and rested with my head against the gnarled mossy wood, my face up to the branches above. Then, slowly, slowly, I looked again. Long dark curls fell in a cascade across wide strong shoulders. And as he stepped from the pool, the water trickling in rivulets down a smooth muscular back, I learned surprise. The water was somehow different, silvery. The hair remained dry. The water - if it was water - beaded, and scurried away from his skin, almost is if it was drawn back to the place it had come from, disappearing down and back to the shimmering surface from where it came. I saw he was naked. He was close enough that I could see the muscles work with every step he took. I could see the skin, and the skin was dry. No trace of the moisture that should have been there remained. I bit my lip, barely daring to breathe.

I knew the pool had no right being here, where days before there had been nothing but open ground. I lowered my basket, careful not to make a sound. Keeping myself low, I stepped between the trees, watching in case he turned, and I found a better vantage point from which to observe.

As he stepped from the pool's edge, he bent then flicked his hair, sending a cascade of drops sparkling in the late afternoon sun. They flew high, and somehow, in the air, took on a life of their own, drawing together into a mass, falling back to the pool, and merging with the flat, shimmering surface. Slowly, languorously, he straightened and turned. I caught my breath, for he was scanning the edges of the clearing, as if he had heard. He stood there confidently, untroubled by his nakedness. I thought to ease backwards, to disappear back into the undergrowth and away from his questing eyes, but something held me. As I watched, barely daring to breathe, he continued his scan, and one hand lazily drifted across his abdomen. Though the action was casual, it was as if he caressed the contours of his firm belly, stirring the thin trail of dark hair growing there. Then he stretched, gave a self-satisfied smile, and rubbed the back of his head before turning away.

My heart beat strongly as I crouched there. I was sure he must have heard me, though he had given no sign. I stood, careful that he remained facing the other way, and stepped slowly back to where I had set my basket.

I took one last look before heading away from the clearing and the pool. He was stretched out on the grass, one leg propped up with an arm behind his head. His dark eyes looked to the sky and there was a knowing smile upon his lips. He could not have seen me, I was sure, but that secret intelligence painted upon his full lips awakened doubt.

The next afternoon I came again, seeking the pool and barely hoping it would be there. A sweet scent hung upon the air, beckoning between the trees. The pool was there even yet, but I could see no sign of the stranger. The water was still, and its clear silvery surface moved only with the traceries of cloud in the sky above. I smoothed down my clothes and stepped into the clearing, looking from side to side, wondering if he might be concealed just as I had been the day before. I wondered who he might be, how the pool had come to be there. Softly I stepped to the water's edge, hesitantly held out a hand, but such strange water I did not dare touch. Only my reflection and the sky peered back at me as I tried to see through its impenetrable depths.

After a time I sat. The trees around me were still. Not the vaguest breeze stirred the sweet scent hanging across the clearing. I stared into the liquid reflections and for a while I thought, then lowered myself to lie and watch the clouds above, just as he had on the previous day. The place was so peaceful. Before long, I closed my eyes.

I know not how, but suddenly I was aware of a presence standing above me. I opened my eyes to stare up into the face of the stranger, the light glowing behind the curling dark hair. Dark eyes looked down upon me from beneath a finely curved brow. His sensuous lips quirked with a smile. The hair around his head fell in ringlets, and despite myself, my gaze traced down his body. He wore nothing more than he had the day before. I bit my lip.

He stood watching me, his legs slightly spaced apart. I did not know what I should do – whether I should scramble backwards and dash for the safety of the trees, or simply stay where I was – so I did nothing. I never thought to utter a word, to question who he was or what he might be doing there. I lay. I watched his face, my heart beating strongly in my chest. All power had been taken from me, but I knew I had made a choice.

His smile grew wider, revealing even white teeth, so strangely white and clean, and he lowered himself to crouch beside me. Still smiling, he reached out, and with his fingers gently pushed the strands of hair away from my brow. My stomach felt empty, hollow with cold excitement. I hardly breathed, and when I did, my breath was ragged. He traced my cheek with the back of his hand. The smell of his skin washed over me, fresh, clean, unsullied by the odours of our people and strangely unfamiliar, scented by something I did not recognize. I lay and watched him, not wanting to move, not wanting to break the spell of what he did. I felt I was in a dream.

He moved his hand to trace my neck, and

then with his forefinger, he drew a line slowly down my chest and to my belly. He lifted his hand and stroked my forehead and the skin around my lips. Where he touched me, my skin tingled. My mouth was dry, and I licked my lips. Gently, he lowered himself to lie beside me. I dared not move, though my heart was pounding, lest the vision dissolve to leave me lying alone in the middle of the clearing. I turned my face to watch him, to trace the contours of his body with my gaze, to drink of him as he lay beside me. There was something painted around the top of one arm. It looked like a set of runes, though of unfamiliar form. I peered, and looking closer, realized that they seemed not painted, but rather as if they were part of his skin. There was no time to wonder more, for my attention was quickly distracted.

Gently, so gently, he continued across my body with his finger — my face, my neck, my chest. I felt my body respond, the warmth growing deep inside me, stirring me. His hand was resting flat now on my belly, and he too was stirring. I could see his manhood growing as he lay there, echoing the feelings that grew in me. Still he made no move but to touch me with his hands, lightly moving them across my middle, then slipping up to cup one breast. His smile was gentle, and despite the strangeness, I returned it.

My breath was coming more rapidly now, and I shifted my thighs to ease my discomfort. I wanted his touch. I wanted his hands beneath me and his body on top of me. I moved my hips, pressing them up towards where his hand rested flat below my navel. Reaching down with both hands, I grabbed my skirts and eased them up, moving my hips from side to side until the cloth was bunched beneath me. He leaned across and pressed his mouth to mine. I pressed my lips against his, questing for the taste of him, fresh, clean, like no taste I had ever had.

Then he was kneeling before me. His eyes held mine and I felt drawn into those depths. I reached up to clasp my fingers behind his neck and pull him down, but he held both my hands and pushed them down and away. Easing my thighs apart, he lowered his face between them. His hands slipped down the outside of my thighs, then worked beneath me, cupping me from below and drawing me to him. I wanted to watch him, to see what he did, but I could do nothing but close my eyes and arch my back. He buried his face between my legs, and with a swallow's touch, his tongue darted down and away. I gasped. Again, that light touch, then stronger. He slipped his tongue across me and pressed down, again, and again. Waves swept across me, and I fell back, a feeble moan escaping my lips with the last of my strength.

He eased his hands from beneath and he withdrew his face. A sweet shudder ran through me, and reluctantly I opened my eyes.

He was gone.

All strength had gone from my limbs, but with some effort I sat up. The clearing was empty, and the pool was smooth and calm. No noise had spoken of his leaving, yet of him there was no sign. I was truly alone. A feeble groan escaped from between my lips.

Though I waited until darkness drew across the woods, he did not return. My legs still weak, I stood and wound back through the trees to my rude dwelling at the edge of the trees.

The next morning I returned, but the clearing was empty. After some time, it was apparent that he would not come. Disappointed, and with dragging step, I left and returned to see to my chores. All through the day, images of the afternoon before danced through my head, and the warm feeling deep in my belly stayed like a slowly burning ember throughout the morning. I could pay no more than half a mind to the tasks at hand; I was waiting eagerly for the afternoon to draw near.

Finally the shadows grew longer, and nervously I returned to the pool, fearing disappointment. Nothing else mattered to me. I did not care how the stranger came to be there. I did not care that I did not know his name, or that not a word had passed between us. I simply wanted to be there, back with him again, and him with me.

As I stepped out into the clearing, he was standing on the opposite side waiting. He looked across at me and smiled, and I smiled back. I stood, not knowing what I would do, and then he took the decision from me. He lifted something before his eyes, then there was a sudden flash of light. When the brightness had gone, and I could see again, whatever he had held was gone. He strode around the edge of the pool to join me. I watched his body move with power and grace, and that feeling of warmth welled up in me again. I wanted him. I wanted his touch.

I opened my mouth to speak, but seeming to anticipate me, he raised a finger and pressed it to my lips. When he seemed assured that I was still, he lowered the hand to my shoulder. Then he lifted his other hand, and with both resting on my shoulders, looked deeply into my eyes. Once more, I was swept away into the depths. All else faded, the clearing, the noises, and the gentle stirring of the breeze through the leaves around us. The afternoon heat was upon my skin, but it paled next to the warmth I felt inside. It seemed as if he was watching me, looking for something, and he tilted his head to one side.

With a sudden pressure on my shoulders, he spun me about. I could feel him behind me. Then, pushing down with his hands, he forced me to my knees. I turned to look at him, but he turned my face to the front, and pushed me down, further, harder, forcing me to bend forwards. He lifted my skirts up around my waist, then slipped a hand down between my legs. I didn't care that I could not see him; I could feel his fingers working between my thighs and I rocked back against him. He pushed me forwards and up again so that I was resting on all fours. Still his fingers worked. I could feel him pressing against me and I closed my eyes. I wanted so much to turn, to touch him, but he held me in place with a hand against my back. The need inside me was growing like a coal and I reached back a hand to draw him to me, but yet again, he pushed it away.

On the verge of crying out, I pressed back, seeking him, and then he was there, pressing hard against me. He slipped inside so smoothly, and his hips pushed forcefully against me, again and again. His fingers knotted in my hair, pulling back my head. I worked my hips with his rhythm, and for a time we moved as one. With a cry, the heat exploded through my body, his and my own. I pitched forwards, lying spread out on the soft grass, able only to muster a whimper, not even caring about the dampness between my legs and on my clothes.

Eventually I turned to find him, to draw him to me and share those few sweet moments of the aftermath, but once more, he had gone. I clutched a handful of grass, as he had clutched my hair, and I tossed it from me. The breeze whipped it away and scattered it on the pool surface, where it floated, the blades spreading slowly. Within moments, those blades picked up speed, skittering to the edge of the pool's surface, as if the pool itself had rejected them.

For seven afternoons I came and for seven afternoons he met me in the fading light. I touched and caressed his lean muscled form and he moved against me, touching me deep within. All throughout, not a single word passed between us. Nor was there a need. Every night and every day, his face, his arms, his hands, floated in my sight, and I knew there could never have been another. He filled me with my hunger — the hunger that stays with me yet.

The eighth day came, and I waited impatiently for the afternoon. I knew that if I went before the day had worn long, he would not be there and that only made the waiting harder.

Finally the hour approached, and with a lightness in my step, I headed for the clearing. Deep within the wooded path, when I was but halfway there, a great sound tore across the sky, a tearing noise, then a loud clap. Birds scattered from the trees. The sound of creatures disturbed and running from the noise came to me from the undergrowth. I stopped and listened, wondering what it might have been. Slowly, the forest stilled. Cautiously, I headed on my way. Nearing the clearing, I strode from the path, no longer cautious, seeking his familiar shape across the pool.

He wasn't there.

The clearing was empty. Gone was the pool. In its place lay a flat expanse, clumps of grass dotted with late summer flowers stretched from end to end. I looked around desperately, barely believing my eyes. I checked the path, hoping perhaps that I had taken a wrong turning, but I knew that I had not. It was the same clearing. I looked around the edges seeking a sign, any sign. Then I saw the mushrooms. They were the very ones I had come to collect a week before, and I knew. Whatever had brought him to me had taken him away. I walked to the centre and stood.

Helplessness washed down upon me, and I slumped, then wept. I wept long into the night. Gently with my fingers, I traced the mushroom shapes, wishing they were something else. The next afternoon I came to that spot, and the afternoon after, but I waited alone except for my tears.

I understand now the old woman's words. For when power gives to you, it also takes away. That which has taken him from me leaves me aching in the still of night and I long for his return.

Next summer, when the days are long, perhaps I will return, and perhaps then, the strangely surfaced pool will return and bring him to me. Though I feared my solitude, though I feared my loneliness, the fear and emptiness has been replaced by yearning. That was the cost of what I did. And though I am alone once more, as I look down and cup my swelling belly, I know that soon, so soon, I will not be alone.

But as I feel the child grow within me, and sense its shape, I wonder. And with that wondering, comes a touch of fear. Perhaps it is the true cost of what I've done.

-The End-

Water's Edge

Waves hissed over thick, coarse sand as they swept back down the beach. Alex squinted out through the oily darkness, yearning for the water's salt sweet touch against his skin. Though he hated the thought, he knew that touch was denied him, not actually, but in a way that mattered. It was a long time now since he'd surged through the waves, cutting through them with the strength of his body, with a body that still had strength.

He shifted his frame awkwardly in his chair and the metal and polymer creaked beneath him. At least his shoulders were still strong. He knew he should really be getting back inside, but the night was warm; he could sit a while longer. No one would be waiting up for him anymore. There was no one left to wait. He'd sit for a while, revelling in the salt tang in his nostrils, the smell of fresh seaweed washed up on the beach, and then, when he was ready, he'd voice the command that whisked the chair back up the twin rails to the house behind. But there was time yet, plenty of time. He closed his eyes and took a deep lingering breath.

The wasting disease had taken his legs first, then most of his motor functions. Strength remained in his upper body, but he'd lost much of the control necessary to use it. If they'd caught the disease earlier, he might have had a chance. All they'd given him instead was fair warning -- enough for him to prepare.

Alex slowly opened his eyes and turned to look back up at the house. His house. It contained everything he needed; everything he would ever need, right until the very end. His ongoing sponsorship deals and the personal fortune he'd amassed while he was still competing had seen to that. Now he had nothing left but the house, and the beach, and enough money to see him through. With a sigh, he turned back to watch the rush and pull of the heaving waves.

He could sit longer in these warm summer nights. In winter, with the leaden grey clouds and white-flecked breakers crashing against the shore, he sat enclosed in the weather field the chair projected around him. Here, like this, open and exposed, he was at one with the water -- he was home, in his true home. He liked it better. He'd never really been a creature of dry land.

Pulling in one last deep breath of the ocean air, he held it, lingering in the moment, before commanding the chair to take him away. He closed his eyes, as he always did, while the chair whizzed back up the slope and inside the house. It whirred to a stop and the broad weather-shield windows slid closed behind him. He turned and slowly opened his eyes. His half-shadowed reflection looked back at him from the window, huddled and crumpled in the chair. He turned his face away from the image -- an image that haunted him every day and night -- and voiced the command that would send the chair to his room to get himself ready for sleep.

oOo

John walked in with a troubled expression on his face. Alex tracked him as he walked slowly into the living room. As soon as he saw his father, the expression quickly faded. He had the strength and good looks, the broad shoulders and dark complexion Alex himself had as a younger man: the very image of his father. Alex just wished the boy had inherited some of his determination and good sense as well.

"Hi, Dad. How are you doing today?" said John, pausing halfway across the room. "Everything all right?"

"Come on in. Don't just stand there," said Alex, marking the hesitation in his son's stance. "I'm fine."

He watched as John took a seat opposite and he adjusted his chair a little to seem him better. "Good to see you. You're looking well ... though a little tired if I may say so. You been working too hard again?"

"No more than usual," John said and shrugged. As he sat, he leaned forward and spent a moment or two subjecting his father to undisguised scrutiny. "Dad, really, how *are* you?"

"I told you, John, I'm fine. But let's not talk about me. It's not as if a lot happens in my life out here. You tell me what you've been up to. How are Maggie and the kids?"

"They're great. Maggie sends her love."

Alex nodded. "I bet they're still growing, eh? So, when are you going to bring them over again? It's been nearly a month."

John avoided his gaze. He let John's silence pass. "Now, how about a drink, eh? Let me get you a drink."

"Yeah, okay."

The trolley whirred into the room, stopped beside John, and the boy took the bottle and poured himself a large scotch. He waved the bottle in Alex's direction, but Alex shook his head.

"So, tell me, what brings you over, John?" he said.

John sipped at his drink and looked out through the windows to the sea stretching beyond the front of the house. He took a long time before answering, chewing at his bottom lip. Finally, he turned back and spoke.

"Yeah, okay. There is something I wanted to discuss with you." He lifted his hand, forestalling any comment. "Dad, before you start, hear me out on this one, will you? I need to talk to you about a project I've been working on."

"Okay...," said Alex, slowly.

"It's just that…well…I really need your help." The words came out in a rush.

Alex felt that hollowness opening up inside. "I don't know what help I can be."

Inwardly, Alex groaned. He might have known. "Are you in trouble again, John? What is it this time? You know I'd do anything to help you and Maggie and the kids.... "

John lifted a hand, then slowly closed his fingers, his lips pressed tightly together. "No, I'm not in trouble exactly. That's not it. We're fine. But yes, -- damn -- I do need money. And please, listen to what I have to say before you start."

Alex lifted his own hand to his forehead. It took an effort to disguise the slight tremor that ran through his arm.

"I knew it," said Alex. "Why now? Look around you, John. This is all I have left. The house, the gadgets, enough to keep me going. That's it. It's about time you understood that."

He glared at John with set jaw, resentful for the string of failures, resentful that it always came to this. And each time, it was like another personal failure.

"It always comes back to money, doesn't it? You know one day all this will be yours anyway. If you're that desperate now, I suppose I could get a loan on all this, the house, the stuff, but I'd have no way of paying it back."

John held his glass between his legs and looked down through it, refusing to meet his father's eyes.

"I just had nowhere else to go," he said quietly. "You've always helped me out in the past. Why not now? This time it's different."

"How is it different, Son? How is it different?" Alex's voice was raised now. "What is this project -- another of your crackpot schemes? Like the last one and the one before that. I've seen too many of them. And now you expect me to..." He spun the chair around and stared out the window, clenching his teeth.

"Jeez, Dad, I thought you'd understand -- you of all people. Knowing how much you love the ocean. I've told you about the project. Or weren't you listening? Think of the benefits. We have the aquaculture all established. We just need to take that decisive step to make the production process efficient. All it needs is that one last injection of capital. Our other sources have run dry. I tried everything before I came to see you. I did. It was hard. I didn't want to, but I only came to you because we're so close I can taste it. And that's not all…"

Alex waited for John to continue, his expression grim, waiting for the latest excuse.

John hesitated, and then continued, slowly, quietly. "This project's special, Dad. There's something I want you to be a part of. It's about time I did something for you."

Alex waited, but there *was* no more. The muffled roar and crash of the breakers was the only sound. Slowly he turned his chair. John sat with his head bowed, but looking up, a hint of expectation in his dark eyes.

"I'm sorry, Son," said Alex after a moment, "but the well's gone dry. I've nothing left to give you."

John stared at him blankly.

"And even if I could, I don't think I would. It's about time you learned to stand up for yourself."

"But you don't understand--"

"I understand well enough. Just like I've understood every time before. No. Not this time, John." He shook his head.

"No," said John. "You really don't understand. You must listen. I'm doing this for you."

"I'm done listening, John. No more handouts."

John made to protest, but Alex cut him off.

"No, I'm done talking. And I really think it's time you left. Come back when you can show me some results. Not before."

"But, Dad --"

"Just leave!" He slammed his hand down on the arm rest and spun his chair around to face the windows again. He heard John get to his feet, place his glass down on the tray and he watched him walk from the room in the vague reflection in front of him. John paused as if to say something else, then shook his head and left the room. Moments later, the front door opened and closed.

Alex spent a long time staring out the window. He knew deep down that this time he'd done the right thing.

oOo

Maggie's image flashed onto the display in front of him and Alex angled the chair to get a better view.

"Maggie! What can I do for you?"

"Alex, I'm sorry for calling. I just thought I should talk to you."

"Not at all. It's always a pleasure to hear from you ... unless ... John hasn't put you up to this, has he?"

"Alex, wait. He'd kill me if he knew I was calling you."

"Well what then? I'm sorry. Please ... go on."

Maggie's dark-bobbed, serious face watched him from the display.

"Well, it *is* John I wanted to talk to you about. He told me about your conversation the other day. He took it pretty hard."

Alex frowned. "What I said was for his own good. He has to learn to look after himself, Maggie. I'm not going to be around for ever."

"But that's just it, Alex. Perhaps you could be. He is doing this for you – that's the point."

Alex narrowed his eyes. "I don't understand."

Maggie leaned closer to the screen. "That's why he didn't want to tell you about it. He wanted to be able to do something for *you* this time, instead. He wanted to surprise you. He has this idea that he can pay you back for everything you've done for us over the years. That's the only reason he came to see you."

She glanced back over her shoulder, then lowered her voice and leaned even closer to the screen. "It has to do with this undersea farming project he's been tied up in. I know he's talked to you about it. The group he's been working with, some of them are involved tangentially in the cybernetic replacement program. You know, the one where they've been using people in the exploration vehicles for planetary surveys -- giving people with no hope an extra chance of life, or that's how they tell it. I know it's a different life, but..."

Alex shook his head. "What has that got to do with me?"

"Listen Alex, how long do you think you've got? Forgive me for saying it, but what sort of life are you leading, stuck in that chair?"

Alex could always count on Maggie to be straight with him. He admired her for that. He could not take offence at her honesty.

"But I told him," said Alex. "There's nothing left. There's enough, maybe, to keep me going for a few years more, and the house, and that's it. I wouldn't lie to you, Maggie."

"I know you wouldn't, Alex. I wasn't saying you would. But there's more to it than that. He's offering you the chance for a new body and a new life. He wants to give you that much. If you agreed, you wouldn't need the house any more. You'd be free of that chair, free of the disease. Think about it."

Alex shifted his weight. If what she was saying was true...

"What assurances would I have? What if it didn't work, if the project didn't get off the ground? We're talking about my life here. I've read about this stuff. They've had problems with it, haven't they? He paused. "There are just too many questions." He shook his head.

"All right, Alex, but think about this. He knew you had very little left when he came to see you. We talked about it before he came and truly, I've never seen him like that before. I could *see* the light in his eyes."

"Just listen, Maggie. I've seen him get all enthusiastic about things before. What about the synthetic fuel project? What about that stupid new engine? What does he have to show for any of it? Nothing."

Her face watched him thoughtfully, shadowed with something deeper. "Look, I have to go now, but think about what I've said. Take some time and think about how much John stands to gain out of this. And please, Alex, promise me you won't let him know I spoke to you."

He stared at the empty space above the desk long time after her image had faded.

Alex turned the chair and looked around at the house, at the devices and the gadgets built in to look after him. So much had gone in to making this place comfortable for him in his declining years. He could be content here until the disease took him beyond the point where he could look after himself, then there'd be little time left anyway.

He needed to think.

He did his best thinking down by the water, and he headed his chair across the living room and out onto the beach. A chill breeze caught his cheeks as he passed the glass doors, but he ignored the weather field. He wanted to be close to the air and water, to feel the spray upon his face, to taste the salt water on the breeze.

Alex felt the tremors in his arm as he lifted his hand to rub his forehead. He knew he didn't have too much longer before the disease really started to take hold. And now—now this.

He lowered his arm and looked up at the sky. John was asking him to risk everything, all for the sake of another one of his hair-brained schemes. Another scheme no doubt doomed to failure.

He dropped his gaze to watch the wave tops. Wasn't it enough that his body had failed him? First John, and now Maggie. He could barely believe that Maggie could simply fall for John's fairy tales again. She normally had such a level head.

What had she said? To think about what John stood to gain. That didn't make sense. The only way he could raise enough funds to give to the project would be to sell the house and all the things that went with it. John would see none of it. He only stood to gain if the project became a success, and with his record...

Slowly, understanding started to dawn. So that was what she had meant. John stood to gain nothing from this. Nothing at all. The project would *have* to work.

He looked out over the waves to the ocean beyond. He watched as a gull soared and dipped above the ocean. For a long time, he stared out at the breakers, listening to them rumble and whisper, knowing the decision he had to make.

oOo

Alex extended the probe and tasted for pollutants, but the water was clean. The sweet salt current swirled past his skin and if he could have shivered, he would have. He kicked his rear rotors into action and soared.

Cutting the rotors, he bumped to a stop just short of the main beds. One by one, he extended his eight legs and flexed them. They eased his heavy body upward and he headed towards the first row of plantings. The crop was coming along well. If he could keep them free of pests for the next month, they should have a good harvest. He was looking forwards to the harvest -- the real chance to flex his muscles.

A school of fish shimmered past and distracted him for a moment, and he tracked them until they disappeared into the green murk of the distance. Then he focused his lenses and increased magnification. The brown, fat, healthy leaves waved gently in the current, and inside, Alex smiled.

Halfway down the first row he paused, thinking about what had happened and thinking about what was to be. He was so happy here. Always the feel and taste of water against his outer skin buoyed his spirits. John had given him so much after all. Alex wondered if he would ever be able to pay him back.

He tilted his lenses back and looked up through the crystal light filtering in shafts through the pale blue ceiling above him. A thin trail of bubbles broke from the ocean floor and swirled slowly upwards through the thin pillars of light. Perhaps eventually he would.

One day, he thought as he smiled inside. There was no other way to smile anymore.

-The End-

About the Author

Hartley James writes science fiction, though sometimes he thinks that the science fiction writes him. Occasionally he writes other stuff. He grew up on speculative fiction of all sorts, though it was the greats, Asimov, Herbert, Dick, Clarke, Wolfe, Heinlein that shaped his perception. In his real life, he does other things, apart from writing, following the principle laid down by Robert A. Heinlein, that specialization is for insects. So, he strives not to be an insect.

Also by Hartley James

The Sirona Cycle

The Jump Point
Daughter of Atrocity
Benevolent

The Serpent Road

Printed in Great Britain
by Amazon

32151578R00152